Dressed in body-hugging leather leggings, and fringed shirt, he looked as if he belonged to a different era. Like his Cheyenne ancestors, colorful beads decorated his shirt and moccasins. He held a knife in one powerful hand. His hair was thick and dark brown, combed straight back like a lion's mane. Jungle-cat green eyes studied her, made her feel exposed. Jane swallowed hard, dropping her own gaze to his powerfully built body.

How he'd changed. But it was Nicholas. She'd know him anywhere, even in a loincloth. He tipped his head, staring at her in puzzlement. He reminded her of Tarzan facing his first woman. And he was just as sexy....

ABOUT THE AUTHOR

Delayne Camp is a veteran romance writer, but this is her premiere Harlequin American Romance. The winner of the first Janet Dailey Award, she lives in Tulsa, Oklahoma.

Books by Delayne Camp

HARLEQUIN TEMPTATION
389—A NEWSWORTHY AFFAIR
435—OKLAHOMA MAN
503—THE BUTLER DID IT

Don't miss any of our special offers. Write to us at the following address for information on our newest releases.

Harlequin Reader Service
U.S.: 3010 Walden Ave., P.O. Box 1325, Buffalo, NY 14269
Canadian: P.O. Box 609, Fort Erie, Ont. L2A 5X3

Taming
The Wild Man

DELAYNE CAMP

Harlequin Books

TORONTO • NEW YORK • LONDON
AMSTERDAM • PARIS • SYDNEY • HAMBURG
STOCKHOLM • ATHENS • TOKYO • MILAN
MADRID • WARSAW • BUDAPEST • AUCKLAND

ISBN 0-373-16598-6

TAMING THE WILD MAN

Copyright © 1995 by Deborah Camp.

Chapter One

He's a cross between Tarzan and Tonto.

Remembering that description of Nicolas Thunderheart, Jane Litton laughed to herself. Her footsteps sounded incredibly loud in the thick wilderness of the Smoky Mountains. Glancing back in the direction she'd left her rental car, she was amazed to see nothing but a blanket of pine needles and towering trees. Anxiety tightened her throat. Would she be able to find her way back?

Nearby, a fallen branch of some four feet leaned against the trunk of a hickory tree. She extracted it from a tangle of vines and a clutch of mushrooms. Perfect for a walking stick, she thought, giving it a try as she trudged farther into the quiet, green world. Nicolas Thunderheart's world. Was she on his land now?

She looked forward to seeing him, although she knew that her ex-brother-in-law wouldn't be thrilled to see her. Well, tough. He'd shirked his duties long enough.

Maybe that was okay with his ex-wife, but it wasn't okay with Jane. She took her responsibilities as aunt and godmother to his only child seriously. He'd never acknowledged Amanda as his own, but Jane was willing to give him the benefit of the doubt. She couldn't help but remember how kind he'd seemed back when he'd married her only sister, Selena. True, Jane had spent precious little time with him, but Selena had painted him as a knight in shining armor and that image lingered in Jane's mind and heart.

Her sister, an up-and-coming opera singer, had warned Jane that Nicolas had changed. He was heartless, self-centered and cared nothing for his daughter, Selena had insisted. But Jane knew people could change. Even Nicolas Thunderheart.

Moving cautiously and trying to make as little noise as possible—it seemed sacrilegious, somehow, to tramp about and raise a ruckus—Jane advanced in the direction indicated by the map she'd found in an architectural magazine. She checked it again, hoping she was translating it correctly. She should be about two miles from Nicolas's unique house.

He'd built it himself, she'd been told. A house constructed across an abandoned trellis bridge and over a gurgling stream. He'd take time to do that, but not to be a father to his child. That did smack of selfishness, she conceded, then told herself to keep an open mind.

She'd developed a crush on him during her college years when she'd been abroad. All the glowing newspaper accounts painting him as a prince of popular causes had fueled her unrequited feelings for her sister's husband. Selena had found it all quite amusing. She'd been young and impressionable back then, Jane thought with an inner shrug.

Selena had written her about the marriage to Nicolas, and Jane had followed his skyrocketing career through the press. She'd become enamored, enchanted. However, his noble business as an ethical investor had gone belly-up six years ago when it was discovered he didn't apply his strict rules to himself. Along with his many other admirers, Jane had felt betrayed. The knight had taken quite a fall off his white charger. But she'd forgive him for all that if he'd only forge a relationship with Amanda.

Morning mist hung at ankle level, obscuring the ground and forcing Jane to wrench her mind back to the present. Her feet churned the swirling fog as she moved deeper and deeper into the forest.

Her steps faltered when she saw a tree that looked familiar. She glanced from it to the walking stick she held. Wasn't this the same place...? She advanced and examined the disturbed vines and mushrooms.

"Rats," she whispered, feeling like a failed Girl Scout. "You're already walking in circles, stupid."

She sat on a blowdown and reviewed the map, frowning at the sketchy directions. Folding the paper, she stuck it back into her pocket. She had to reach his place by sundown or she'd be forced to make camp. Glancing around her, she smothered a shiver that tried to shake her confidence.

Sighing, she leaned back on stiff arms and admired the beauty around her. Leaves whispered and sky-high branches groaned softly in the breeze. A black beetle ran over Jane's hiking shoe and hurried across a carpet of pine needles and crushed leaves. She filled her lungs with the cool, stinging air. She identified the heady aroma of pine, and the musky perfume of damp earth, moss and wild vegetation.

Tipping back her head, she watched the flight of a large bird...an eagle! Her heart soared with it, and she feasted on the rare sight of the majestic raptor. With an impressive wingspan, it drifted overhead, silent and omnipotent.

"Oh, you gorgeous thing," she whispered, awed. She'd seen eagles only in books and on film. As the bird circled overhead, she remembered her camera in her backpack. For an instant, she thought to retrieve it, but figured the eagle would be long gone by that time. He was already widening his circle, almost slipping from her limited view.

She heard a click and instinctively looked toward the sound. Then an explosion startled her so, that she fell backward off the log, her ears ringing, her nose catching the acrid scent of spent gunpowder. The eagle screamed, and Jane looked up, her heart climbing into her throat. The august bird flapped wildly, then righted itself and soared higher, out of sight.

Using the walking stick, Jane pushed herself to her feet and whirled in the direction of the gunfire. A man stood no more than twenty paces from her, his black-and-red-checked wool hat pulled down so low that it folded the tops of his ears. One moment he was there, and the next he was gone, swallowed by branches and bushes. Jane listened to his footfalls until they grew faint. Only then did she release her pent-up breath. She flexed her cramped fingers, realizing that she'd been gripping the walking stick as if it were a lifeline...or a weapon with which to defend herself.

Relaxing, she let her mind catch up with events. She'd just witnessed a crime! It was illegal to shoot eagles. What could she do to make sure he wouldn't get another chance to—

Something bowled her over. Something big. Something that moved on silent feet. One moment she was standing, and the next, she was lying flat on the ground. The breath whistled out of her, and her lungs seemed to collapse under the weight of her attacker.

Suddenly she was flipped over. Something cold pressed against her throat. She saw stars for a few moments, and realized she was gasping for air. The clothing, toiletries and camera in her backpack poked at her spine and shoulders.

She heard a vicious growl and heavy breathing above her. Her vision cleared enough for her to see a man bent over her, but she couldn't make out his features. She was aware of shaggy hair and buckskin.

He held something against her throat. She felt an edge, and knew it was a knife. Her eyes must have telegraphed her fear and confusion, because he straightened and removed the blade from against her tender skin.

"Just what the hell do you think you were doing?" he asked, his voice punctuated by his overwrought breathing. "Don't you know that it's illegal to shoot eagles?" He glanced around. "What did you do with that rif—" He snapped his jaws shut and let go of her down-filled vest to grab her walking stick. "Well, I'll be damned," he whispered, his voice rife with chagrin. "I thought this was a rifle. If you didn't fire on that eagle, who did?"

She gulped for air, finally finding enough to inflate her lungs. He eased his big body off hers. The relief was immediate. Jane sucked in another great breath, which cleared her vision and swept the haziness from her mind. She levered herself to a sitting position and pushed her long, blond hair back from her face.

"I didn't shoot anything. The guy who did was here just a sec—" Her words skidded to a halt as her eyes took in the living, breathing fantasy before her.

He was big and beautiful. Dressed in body-hugging leather leggings and fringed shirt, he belonged to a different era. Native American beads decorated his shirt and moccasins. He held a wicked bowie knife in one powerful hand—the knife that had been pressed against her throat only moments ago. His hair was thick and dark brown, combed straight back like a lion's mane. Jungle-cat green eyes studied her, made her feel exposed. Jane swallowed hard, dropping her own gaze to his powerfully built body.

How he'd changed! Old photos had shown him as a smiling, young businessman, his hair carefully combed. But it was him. She'd know him anywhere, anyhow, even in a loincloth.

"Kindly help me up, Nicolas."

He rose to his feet and tipped his head, staring at her in puzzlement. He reminded her of Tarzan facing his first woman. "I'm Jane." She stuck out her hand, but resisted the rest of the movie dialogue. "You're Nicolas Thunderheart. I just now recognized you."

He gripped her hand and hauled her to her feet. "You look familiar, but I can't place..."

"I was your sister-in-law, once upon a time." She ran her gaze over him. "I didn't expect to find you dressed like . . . well, Tonto."

He recovered quickly. His eyes widened, then narrowed to dangerous slits. "Jane? What the hell are you doing here, besides trespassing?"

"I'm here to see you."

"I can't imagine why, and I don't remember inviting you."

He moved to brush past her, but she snagged the fringe dangling from his sleeve. "Hey, wait a minute."

"Why? Is Selena hiding somewhere back there?" he asked, almost growling at her as he slipped the bowie into a sheath hanging from his belt. He peered past her into the green-and-brown landscape.

"No. I came alone. I want to talk to you."

He gave her a quick once-over. "You don't look anything like Selena."

"We had different fathers."

"Oh, that's right. I forgot." He cleared his throat and looked past her again, then raised a hand to point. "Walk due east and you'll come upon the highway. Good hiking."

She tightened her hold on his leather sleeve. "Not so fast, big guy." She ignored his arched brow and pointed glare at her detaining hand. "I'm sorry to be raining on your parade, but I'm not leaving. You can be rude and I'll still have my say."

He sighed, hung his hands at his hips and shook his head. "Let's get to the point. I know why you're here, and I'm not interested."

He covered her hand with his, and she was struck by how small hers felt under his—how tiny *she* felt beside him. At five feet nine, she wasn't used to looking up at men, but she found herself tipping up her chin to see Nicolas Thunderheart's dark green eyes. He swept her hand off his sleeve, pivoted sharply and left her in his dust.

Fury rose in Jane like bile. She stomped after him, as determined as a foxhound after catching the scent. She would not allow him to turn his back on his primary responsibility another day! And what had she ever done to deserve such treatment? A niggling worry grew within. Was Selena right, after all?

He plowed confidently through the brush, his big body moving with an eerie grace, his moccasined feet making hardly a rustle. Jane, on the other hand, sounded like a herd of buffalo on the run.

"I'm not like Selena in many ways," she called ahead to him. "I won't let you walk off without a backward glance. You're going to listen to me. And I don't feel sorry for you. You got what you deserve when you lost your business and your good name."

Satisfaction was hers as he swung slowly back toward her, reluctance in every movement. *Gotcha,* she thought, congratulating herself for finding his Achilles' heel.

He came back to her, his long legs eating up the distance. Jane stood her ground with difficulty. He was better looking than she remembered, more magnificent than she'd dreamed. Leather laces adorned the front of his shirt, and through their crisscrossing, she spied a sprinkling of springy dark hair on his chest. A primitive yearning broke loose inside of her. She curled her fingernails into her palms and shook her head, dazzled by him. She felt as if she'd been thrown back a hundred years—a blue-blooded damsel facing her first Native American.

"I never asked for anyone's pity." He stopped before her. "What has Selena been telling you?"

"I talk better when I've got my feet up and my backside planted in a comfortable chair."

"Is that so? And why should I accommodate you? No one invited you here."

"Common courtesy, Nicolas. I think it's the least you can do after throwing me to the ground and putting a knife to my throat. While I wasn't physically harmed, there is a chance that the camera in my backpack was smashed when you sat on me." She brushed leaves and grass off her khaki pants. "Therefore, I don't think it's a lot to ask that you offer me a smidgen of hospitality, especially since we used to be family."

His gaze took its time moving from her face down the length of her body and back up. A smile nudged one corner of his wide mouth. Jane felt like a prey brought to ground, but she hoped it didn't show.

His chest expanded impressively as he gathered in a deep breath. "Okay, you win. I'm going home. If you can keep up, fine. If not..." He shrugged. "Hope you brought a compass." With that, he turned and slipped through the woods like morning mist.

Jane hurried after him, making noise in his silence, stumbling in his sure-footed prints and barely keeping him in sight. He moved quickly, efficiently, knowingly, like an animal. She noticed new things about him—his carved walking stick, his black breechcloth, which flapped occasionally to give her a glimpse of his lean hips, and the shaggy cut of his hair, as if it had been lopped off with a knife instead of styling scissors.

She judged that he was about five or six inches above six feet tall, and more than two hundred pounds, all long muscles and lean sinew. Damn him, he was fascinating! Just watching him tread lightly through the woods made her blood run hot. Selena had told her that he often wore Native American-style clothing, but Jane hadn't been prepared for the impact of being pounced on by a man straight out of a leatherstocking tale!

"Hey, there," she called out to him. "Were you going to slit that guy's throat—the one who shot at the eagle?"

"No, but I was hoping to scare the hell out of him," he called back. "And I was going to haul his butt to the game warden's office in town."

"Town? You mean Asheville?" she asked, naming the closest pocket of North Carolina civilization.

"That's right. Is that where you're staying?"

"Actually, I was hoping to stay with you."

That stopped him. He waited for her to catch up. "You'd bunk alone with me? We hardly know each other. You're that trusting?"

Having always thought of herself as being physically fit, it was with great distress that Jane had to bend, hands propped on her knees, and seize the moment to regain her breath. Her lungs burned; her throat and mouth felt as if they were coated with oatmeal. She glanced up at him. An arrow of sunlight blazed through the tree branches to put sparkles in his eyes.

"From what Selena told me, you're nothing to worry about," she said, aiming at his male ego.

"Don't believe everything you're told," he rejoined, devils dancing in his eyes.

Jane straightened to stretch her aching back muscles. "You've already attacked me and I survived."

A smile threatened one corner of his mouth. "True enough. Well, come on. Let's make tracks."

She looked past him at trees and more trees. "How much farther?"

"You don't *look* out of shape," he noted, eyeing her with a slight grin.

She wanted to tell him that she jogged two miles every day and had a membership at a health club. But she couldn't lie. While she thought of herself as in shape, she had never been one to exercise religiously.

Unable to withstand his chiding, Jane looked down at her scuffed shoes. When she looked back up, he was already ten paces ahead of her. She followed the trail he blazed.

Jane tried to ignore the little voice inside that questioned her motives. Maybe this wasn't her fight. Maybe she was being too nosy, taking her rights as a godmother and aunt too seriously. Maybe this had more to do with how her own father had chosen to ignore her, even after she'd contacted him, wearing her heart on her sleeve.

Stop it! another voice inside her demanded. She had every right to be here, to confront this man. She happened to love his daughter with all her heart, and it galled her that he'd gone five years without ever once calling or writing Amanda.

Jane's own father—But that was another story and had nothing to do with this. This was all for Mandy.

"Welcome to the bridge to nowhere, as Selena called it," Nicolas announced, diving into her thoughts, making her mind come up for air. Her legs trembled, and she realized she'd walked a great distance while trying to convince herself that her mission was noble.

Jane stumbled to a halt and looked up from her careful study of the terrain. She heard the gurgle of a swiftly moving stream and the raucous call of a crow, then she saw the house and her knees nearly buckled.

Chapter Two

"It's more than I imagined," she whispered, then realized that Nicolas had hold of her elbow and forearm to keep her upright. She laughed at her exaggerated reaction and regained her equilibrium. "Forgive me, it's just that ever since I heard about this house and beautiful land—well, let's just say I'm spellbound."

Lifting her elbow from his cupped hand, she edged away from him, embarrassed by her emotional display. She moved forward, drawn by the interesting abode stretching across a rock-strewn, bubbling stream. The main floor was built upon a trestle bridge, long abandoned. On either end of the bridge, he'd built two-story additions with rock walls and generous windows. The whole house blended into the surroundings, all subtle shapes and natural colors.

Towering pines, willows and cottonwoods stood sentry along the stream and created green canopies for the house so that it sprawled in cool shadows. She already knew that he owned fifty acres. Selena had also told her this house was seven miles from the highway and twenty-four from Asheville. But her sister hadn't told her how serenity seemed as much a part of this place as the bird songs or the babble of the stream.

Jane felt a connection and was reminded of her childhood visits to her grandfather's Ozark farm. Dallas was a distant place, and she didn't care if she ever saw it again.

"You're lucky," she said without thinking. She glanced at Nicolas and was glad that he wasn't looking at her as if she were crazy.

"Seeing it and living it are two different things." He smiled and extended a hand. "After you."

"Thanks." She moved eagerly toward the house, taking it all in—the work shed built beneath a spreading elm, the numerous bird feeders and birdhouses, the vegetable garden in raised beds and cold frames, protected by chicken wire and tomato cages. "It must be wonderful to be self-sufficient."

He studied her expression carefully before he answered. "You really do like my home, don't you?"

"Oh, yes," she assured him. "To me, this looks like heaven on earth." What a pity he never shared it with his daughter, she thought, and her feelings toward him hardened.

He escorted her to the front door, pausing to wipe his feet on a mat of woven grass. Pulling a key from a leather pouch hanging from his belt, he unlocked the nondescript door. A ship's bell hung to one side. The doorbell, Jane presumed.

"Come on inside. I'll give you a quick tour, but don't expect too much. I live simply."

She stepped inside quickly while the invitation was still good. The front foyer was a mudroom, good for removing soiled shoes, overcoats, sweaters, rain gear.

"Let me help you with your backpack."

She shrugged out of the straps. His hands rested briefly on her shoulders before skimming down her arms. Gentle hands. He put the backpack on a table, then surprised her by flipping her hair back over her shoulders.

"That's a load off, isn't it?"

She nodded and cleared her throat of nerves. "That backpack felt as light as a feather early this morning, but it was beginning to feel like a block of cement." She unzipped it and checked on her camera.

"Is it broken?"

"Doesn't seem to be. That's a miracle. I thought for sure—uh-oh . . ." She withdrew a white shirt streaked with beige liquid. "I think my bottle of makeup is broken in there somewhere."

"You don't need to wear makeup, anyway."

"Neither do my clothes."

He chuckled. "Leave that and come see the rest of the house."

The only other room on that level was a library-den. Jane caught a glimpse of built-in bookshelves and comfortable furniture before following Nicolas up a flight of stairs which emptied into a big, country kitchen with double ovens and a glass-fronted refrigerator, the kind used in restaurants—except that this one was compact.

"Oh," she whispered, admiring the kitchen. "I'm in love."

He smiled. "You like to cook?"

She nodded. "This is a cook's dream! Makes me itch to knead some bread dough or whip up some cookies."

He folded his hands over his heart and feigned a swoon. "That's sweet-talking to this man. We'd better get out of here before we do something we'll both regret—like stir-fry or flame broil." He gave her a good-natured wink.

Jane blinked, astounded by his humor and her desire to give in to it. Wouldn't it be nice if he had a perfectly good reason for not seeing Amanda....

She trailed behind him, and tried not to enjoy the view of his flapping breechcloth and buckskin-bound legs, but it was impossible. He was a looker, all right. And she loved the way he moved. Liquid, languid, lithe, sexy as hell. No wonder Selena had fallen hard and fast. They'd only known each other two weeks before getting married.

"This is the living room and dining room. We're over the stream in these rooms. I've tucked another library over here," he said, moving across the long, narrow area to a wall of shelves. "I read a lot. I have a television, but I don't watch much. News programs and sports. The reception is terrible." He shrugged, his hand moving over the top of an occasional table arranged beside a comfortable wing chair and pedestal lamp.

The dining area opened into the living room. The furniture was simple, reminiscent of the Shaker designs. Oil lamps lined a mantel in the dining room, candles lined the one in the living room. On either side, the walls were glass, giving an unparalleled view of the Smoky Mountain majesty.

"No curtains, no blinds, no shutters?" she observed, standing before a bank of double-thick windows.

"Who would I be worried about seeing inside my home?" he asked. "Squirrels, birds, possums?"

She smiled. "Yes, you're right. I'm used to a city with a million prying eyes." She looked past him to an open doorway. "And what is in the other addition?"

"Bedrooms are on this level, and my office area is downstairs. Oh, there's a bathroom through there, too."

She smiled. "That's a relief. I thought you'd have an outhouse."

He smiled back. "I do. The bathroom has a chemical toilet. I use the outhouse as much as possible." He moved to look out at the green kingdom. "I don't know if you noticed, but there aren't any power or telephone lines out here, or any plumbing." He tipped his head forward to scrutinize her. "Still love the thought of being self-sufficient?"

"What do you do for water?"

"I pump it from the stream. I have a generator for electricity. The refrigerator has its own generator, but I usually turn it off during the winter and use nature's cold to keep my perishables from spoiling. Of course, I don't keep many perishables." He sighed. "It sounds complicated, but it isn't. Just common sense."

"I suppose it would take some getting used to, but I do believe I would love the solitude."

He lowered his brows, clearly perplexed. "You sure don't sound like a city girl."

"Guess I'm a country girl at heart." She spread out her arms. "I love this house. You're a genius to think of building it over the stream."

"Not really. I saw a house like this once before, and I never forgot it. When I found this land and bridge, I snapped it up." He ran a hand down his leather shirt. "Now, if you'll excuse me for a few minutes, I'll change clothes. Now that I'm back home, I feel funny in this getup."

She studied him, hearing something in what he'd said. Now that he was back home... "You mean, you don't usually dress like that?"

"What?" He gave her a startled look, then chuckled. "You thought I dressed like this all the time? Hell, no! I've been to a rendezvous."

"A what?"

"Rendezvous," he repeated. "It's a reenactment—a retreat for people who like to live the way their ancestors did a century ago. There's one at the old reservation this week, and I went to it yesterday to see some friends. Spent the night with them in their lodge and hiked back home this morning." He chuckled again. "And you thought I was a real wild Indian, huh? Running around with my loincloth flapping in the breeze." He tipped back his head and laughed until his eyes watered. "Oh, that's rich."

"How was I to know? I just thought you'd gone native out here on your lonesome."

"Well, sorry to disappoint you, but this is a costume, which I'm going to change out of now." He motioned toward the sofa and chairs. "Make yourself comfortable."

"Thanks, I will." She turned to look out the windows again.

Nicolas left her there before the bank of glass and went to his room to change into jeans and a T-shirt. What the hell was she doing here? he wondered. He could barely remember her. In fact, if he wasn't mistaken, they'd met at the wedding briefly and then once more over Christmas holidays. She must have been about nineteen and home from Oxford where she'd gone on scholarship. A light bulb went off in his head. She'd been a communications major! That's why she was snooping around. She smelled a good story.

Too bad she was related to Selena. If she weren't, he might have extended her time here, letting her think he might cooperate on having his life smeared all over the newspapers again while he enjoyed the pleasure of her smile and the huskiness of her voice. He'd spied intelligence in her eyes and he admired her grit, standing up to him when he'd acted like a glowering bear.

After all this time, why seek him out now? He'd heard nothing from Selena or any of her family, and he hadn't cared. But now her kid sister shows up, wanting to spend some time with him, to talk. About what? She *had* to be after a story. There could be no other reason for her sudden appearance after all this time.

When he joined her again, she was as he'd left her, standing by the windows, staring out, a slight smile flirting with her mouth. Stunning woman, he thought, admiring her lithe figure and golden tan. While Selena had always looked dark and voluptuous, Jane was all golden and athletic.

"Do you have any neighbors?" she asked.

He nodded in a vague direction. "Abby Masters. She lives on my land. She's a botanist, and a fair cook." He headed for the kitchen. "How about a cool drink of lemonade?"

"That's sounds wonderful. Well, have you decided?" she asked, following him into the kitchen.

"About what?"

"Me spending the night here."

He held up a single finger. "One night. By the time I got you packed up and back to the highway, it would be dusk. I'll see you to the highway in the morning." He handed her the glass of lemonade.

"One night is fine. I'll be happy to hit the road in the morning after I've appeased my curiosity."

He took a drink of the tart juice, wondering if he should believe her. Did she think he'd quickly agree to an interview? Maybe she thought she could bat her lashes, remind him they used to be family and watch him cave in. Obviously, she didn't know him well. Although...perhaps she did have an understanding of the male animal. He sniffed, fancying he could smell her. Musky, sweet, like a moss rose. Sunlight fell across her face, throat and chest, gilding her, caressing her. He cleared his throat, uneasy with the direction his thoughts were taking him. Be civilized, he cautioned himself, and quit acting like this is mating season.

"Jane," he sounded her name, then wondered if she might be married. "Jane, what?"

"Litton."

"So you *are* married."

She shook her head, smiling.

"Divorced?"

Another shake of her head and a playful frown.

"But... Litton. Selena's maiden name is—" He stopped himself, recalling her parentage. "Oh, right. Different fathers. I keep forgetting that."

She gave a wink and pointed a finger at him. "I knew you'd figure it out—eventually."

He grinned. "You're a good-looking woman." Had he said that? "Different from Selena," he added, but his mouth kept going, the words falling out before he could stop them. "A beauty in your own right."

Damn, she must think he was full of lines! Nicolas turned away and grabbed the lemonade pitcher. He topped off his glass, feeling his face grow warm.

"I hope that didn't sound like I'm coming on to you," he muttered, then winced. Hell, there was no way out of this!

She laughed, lightly. "Guess you don't get many women visitors out this way, huh, Nic?"

He chuckled, glad that she was making a joke of it. Facing her again, he hoisted his glass in a salute and decided to join in. "You asking me if it's been a while?"

"No." The smile slipped from her lips and bright color infused her face. "I... of course I'm not asking. That is... I'm not coming on to you, either."

He took a long drink of the lemonade and set the glass aside. Somehow he didn't believe her, no more than he believed that he wasn't flirting with her. If he wasn't yet, he was definitely working up to it.

"Now that we've determined neither one of us wants anything to do with the other, why don't you shoot straight and tell me why you're here."

"I thought it was time someone from my family talked to you, and since Selena won't, I drafted myself."

"How noble. I wasn't feeling left out, though. While I always liked your mother, I never expected any of Selena's family to throw out the welcome mat for me after the divorce."

"But divorce doesn't always mean a complete severance from every member of the family," she ventured, her tone hesitant as if she were choosing each word carefully.

He studied her. What was she getting at? "Uh, right. It doesn't have to mean that." He shrugged, completely befuddled, but she seemed to like his answer because her eyes sparkled and her lips formed a pretty smile.

Feeling suddenly like a lion confronted with a most cunning tamer, Nicolas stretched his arms above his head and dragged his fingertips across the peaked ceiling. He needed room . . . space—he needed to get away from her guileless charm. "I'll show you to the spare bedroom, if you want."

She nodded. "I'd like that."

He led the way again with her on his heels as persistent as a pup. The guest room was sunlit with twin pencil-post beds and matching bureau and wardrobe in the Shaker style. Skylights provided an open ambience. He saw her studying it and figured she was wondering who, if anyone, ever used it.

"My brother visits occasionally, and a few past associates from my glory days." Now why had he volunteered that? he asked himself crossly. She didn't deserve any tidbits of his life.

"Oh, yes. I remember hearing about your brother. He stayed with you and Selena for a while, didn't he?"

"Yes, after our parents died." Nicolas retreated, wanting to escape and be alone with his thoughts. "Okay, so if there's anything you need, just give a shout and I'll—"

"Don't be so quick to be rid of me," she admonished. "You want to know why I'm here, right? You have no idea why I'd track you down?"

He inched back his head to regard her from his height advantage. "Track me down? I haven't been hiding."

"You're not exactly on the beaten path, either," she observed, sitting on the edge of one bed and giving a little bounce to test the mattress. She swung to him, her expression suddenly sad. "This place is so beautiful, so perfect, and such a waste."

"Waste?" He blinked in confusion. "I thought you said it was heaven."

"It could be," she amended. "And you could be a nice guy—a knight in shining armor."

He folded his arms against his chest, disconcerted by this train of conversation. If she wasn't coming on to him, then what was all this romantic idealism talk? "Believe me, a knight in armor I could never be."

"You were once," she whispered, rising up to face him. "I remember when I was in college and I thought you were an example of the 'handsome American.' I was in England."

He nodded. "Oxford."

"That's right, and I heard a lot about the 'ugly American.' I followed your career through the media. I admired you. Everyone did. I even had a little crush on you, I think." She avoided his eyes for a moment. "Anyway, the point is, I believed in you. I believed you had a good heart and that you wouldn't do anything as callous as turning your back on your ethics or your family. But all this time, all these years, and not one word." Her voice had risen and she visibly fought to control it. "Selena is content to allow you to ignore your family, but I can't."

"Family?" Nic made a scoffing sound that brought bright flags of color to her cheeks. "Look, Selena filed for divorce, remember?" He retreated another step, nonplussed. Why was she talking about family and Selena in the same breath? "By the time my business went belly-up, we'd decided that ours was not a match made in heaven." He glanced around at the sunny room. "Even in *this* heaven. Where Selena is concerned, my conscience is clear."

"I'm not talking about Selena," she said, teeth gritted.

He sat on the other bed, his hands dangling between his knees, weariness weighting him as the charade lost all its luster. "Let's get down to it, shall we?" He sought out her warm brown eyes. "You're here as a professional. Don't bother to deny it. I do remember what you majored in at college—journalism. You're a reporter, right? You're here to get a story. Well, sorry.

I have no intention of giving you one. Not even for a sweet-talking member of my ex-family."

Jane folded her arms in front of her and stared him down. "Wrong. Dead wrong."

"Oh?" Nic quirked a brow. "Which part?"

"All of it."

"You didn't major in journalism?"

"I did, but I changed careers. If I remember correctly, I'm not the only one. Didn't you major in Native American history? You were going to be a college professor, weren't you?"

He pushed his hair back off his forehead in an agitated gesture. Did she have a dossier somewhere on him? Standing, she moved toward the doorway. "You have a memory like an elephant."

"About some things, yes."

"Teaching wasn't my thing, so I took a job with an investment firm," he confessed. "Before I knew it, I'd found my niche."

"Well, reporting wasn't *my* niche. I realized that after working a year on a daily newspaper in Austin."

"So what do you do now, besides tracking down ex-brothers-in-law?" He held up one hand, palm out, and shook it urgently as his weariness gave way to a vein of foolishness. "Wait, wait! You're a process server, right?" He winked at her, getting a spark of temper from her. "You're damn good at it, too, I bet." He shook his hand again in midair to stop any acidic comment from her. "Or maybe you're a bounty hunter. You always get your man."

"Ha. Ha. I'm dying of laughter." She didn't crack a smile. "I'm a jewelry designer."

Nic's mouth fell open, then he snapped it shut. What the hell . . . ? "I'm at a loss," he said, laughing under his breath as he glanced at his unadorned fingers. "I don't know why a jewelry designer would want to get ahold of me. I'm not much for rings and other baubles. Did someone—Selena, perhaps—suggest I might have money to invest in your business? If so, then I'm sorry to dis—"

"You're way off target, Tonto." She stood and faced him.

"Am I?" He studied her with narrowed eyes, thinking to tell her to stop with her nicknames, but then deciding not to rise to that particular bait. If she wasn't a reporter, then what? Didn't she say something about . . . ? He grinned and took a few slow steps toward her as if he were stalking his prey. He might be thinking with some other part of his anatomy besides his brain, but perhaps the lady protested too much. "Jane, I believe you said something about having a crush on me."

She opened her mouth in shock.

"Did you come here to see if I was everything you'd read about? Didn't you believe Selena when she said I was no good?" He reached out to finger a strand of her wheat-colored hair. "You should have heeded big sis's words of warning, Jane. You're bound to be disappointed." He studied her face with the intensity of an artist viewing a nude form and his mouth went dry as a fire licked beneath his skin. God, she was beautiful!

With a jerk of her head, Jane snatched the lock of hair from his caressing fingers. "Don't flatter yourself, Tonto."

"You can call me Nic," he purred, enjoying the interplay, even though he now strongly suspected he was way off base.

"And you can cool your jets." She backed toward the bed. "I didn't come here to romance you. As a matter of fact, I came here to nail your hide to a fence post."

He spread a hand across his chest. "For what?"

"For turning your back on the best thing in your life." She gave him a haughty glare before that unaccountable sadness fell across her face again. "Selena's right," she whispered, more to herself than to him. "She always told me that your daughter would be better off without ever seeing you, without ever knowing you, and I must agree with her."

For a blazing moment, Nic couldn't move, couldn't breath, couldn't think. One word buzzed in his head like an angry wasp, stinging him over and over. She was moving away from him, dismissing him. Blindly, he reached out and wrapped his fingers tightly around her wrist. He spun her back to face him. Her eyes widened when his gaze slammed into her.

"Let go of me!" She clawed at his hand on her wrist, frantic to be free of him.

But she wasn't going anywhere. Not until she repeated that word so that there was no mistaking it. A cold, clammy sweat coated his skin and his voice came out hoarse, raw, almost savage.

"I'm only going to ask you this once, and I want an answer. No games, no empty threats." Nic drew in a sharp breath that seared his lungs and sliced through his laboring heart. *"What daughter?"*

Chapter Three

He's bluffing, she told herself. *And I won't fall for it.* Jane arched a brow and regarded Nic with open skepticism.

"So you expect me to believe that you never knew about your daughter?" Jane fashioned a smirk. "Sorry. I'm not buying that."

"Look, lady, I'm not trying to sell you anything. *You're* the one who's staging a big snow job here." A muscle ticked in his jawline and it didn't take a psychic to feel his quivering outrage.

He's good, she thought. If she didn't know better, she'd swear he was ready to spit nails. Hey, maybe he was! Maybe he was furious that someone had finally tracked him down and pinned him to the mat.

"Did *she* tell you this or did you think this little scam up all by yourself?"

"By she, do you mean Selena? My sister doesn't even know I'm here."

He advanced. She retreated. "What do you want, lady? Give it to me straight."

"I want you to stop pretending you don't know anything about your daughter." She bunched her hands into tight fists and thrust her face up to his. "I want to hear you admit that you're wrong to turn your back on her and that you'll include yourself in her life from now on."

He shook his head slowly, then with more conviction. "Selena told you this, right? She had some guy's child and said it was mine. You believed her. Hell, she's probably convinced everyone. She certainly has a flair for the dramatic." He barked a hollow laugh. "The great opera singer. Her career has taken off, hasn't it?"

Jane nodded. "And deservedly so. Life hasn't been a picnic for my sister, but she's done well for herself *and* for her daughter. She's been sought by major opera companies and she's always busy these days."

He ran an unsteady hand through his hair and a heavy, silky lock curled onto his wide forehead. "I can't believe this. You prance in here and tell me I have a child. After all this time . . . How old is the kid?"

"The kid," Jane said through clenched teeth, "is five."

"Five." He stared blankly at her. "A girl."

"That's right. A girl." She hoped he'd drop the injured-party act soon. Disappointment hit her in the gut. Why didn't he accept the blame?

"I thought it was about time you were forced to acknowledge you're a father. Selena told me you'd be like this, but I had to see for myself." She raked him with a glare she hoped singed. "Well, I've had *my* eyes opened. And you can quit grinding your teeth and looking pitiful. I have no sympathy for you."

"This had better be a lie," he said, his voice low and throbbing. "Because if you're telling the truth, if I have a daughter no one bothered to inform me about *for five years,* then somebody's going to pay—big time.''

Suddenly the room seemed no larger than a postage stamp and Nicolas took up most of it. Jane glanced around, feeling unbalanced and no longer so certain he was putting on an act. A ragged, torn chord quavered in his voice and he breathed unevenly as he rubbed his face vigorously. She heard the scrape of whisker stubble against his palms.

"What's her name?" he asked, his eyes suddenly bloodshot.

"Amanda Jane."

His lips formed the name, but he didn't speak it. "Selena says she's mine? Has she told others this besides you?"

Jane shrugged. "She doesn't broadcast it, but it's never been any secret."

He turned his back on her and uttered a vicious oath. "I can't believe this. Why would she...it doesn't make sense. None of it makes any sense."

"You told her you didn't want children."

"That's right." He spun to face her again. "I didn't want any with our marriage limping along. We were miserable, and I had proved I was no 'father knows best' with Richie, my kid brother."

Jane sat on the edge of the bed and curved one hand around one of the smooth wood posts. Vague memories of his brother materialized in a far corner of her mind. He'd been given custody of Richie after their parents died. Selena hadn't been happy with that turn of events. Her sister and Nic's brother hadn't gotten along and Richie had lived with them for only a brief time.

"Neither one of us was ready to become parents," Nicolas continued, pacing to the window, then back to the door. He reminded Jane of a caged tiger.

"Selena couldn't be as pragmatic," Jane noted. "She had to *get* prepared once she discovered she was pregnant."

"Was this before or after we separated?"

"You're saying you don't know?"

He whipped around to her, rage stamped clearly on his handsome face. "I'm saying that whether you're lying or telling the truth, you've got a lot of explaining to do, lady."

She narrowed her eyes, incensed by his tone. "I have a name and it's not 'lady.'"

"So do I, and it's not Tarzan or Tonto." He made a dismissive gesture, his big hand slicing through the air inches from her nose. To her intense irritation, she blinked.

"If you're lying, then I want to know why and what kind of payment you expected to extract from me," he demanded. "If you're not lying, then I've been denied my own child since her birth and there's going to be hell to pay."

"Are you threatening me?" Jane asked, her voice not as strong as she'd hoped.

He leaned closer, his eyes darkening to black. "Are you lying to me, Jane Litton?"

Her pulse pounded in her ears, sounding like hail on an empty oil drum. "No, Nicolas, I'm not."

He scoured her face with his hard gaze before straightening and heading out of the room.

"Wh-where are you going?"

"I've got work to do." He paused on the threshold and gripped the large ring that served as a door handle. "I'm not sure I believe you. I've got to think about this."

"Why would I lie?"

He shrugged one shoulder. "Why would *I*?"

"Because you never wanted a child . . . or you don't want to spend any of your precious time or money on one . . . or you're a child yourself and can't stand the competition."

He cocked his head and pretended to listen intently as he tracked the room with his crafty eyes. "Hmm. I could have sworn I just heard Selena's voice. Guess it was only a pale imitation." One corner of his mouth quirked as he pulled the thick door shut behind him.

Pale imitation, indeed! Jane sat heavily on the bed and struggled with her temper. She glanced around the sparsely appointed room with its white eyelet curtains and bedsheets. "Well, I'm here," she whispered, attempting to gain some satisfaction for at least reaching that goal.

With a sigh, she investigated the room and adjoining dressing room, then realized that she'd left her things downstairs. She opened the door to go get them, only to find her duffel bag sitting directly outside the guest bedroom. Jane glanced up and down the hall, but no one stirred. The man walked on feathers, she thought as she carried her bag inside and unpacked her toiletries. She cleaned up the messy makeup and checked out her other items. All seemed unharmed.

Crossing the room to one of the windows, she pulled aside the curtain and found herself admiring a spreading oak, so close to the house Jane estimated she could reach out, grab a limb and shimmy to the ground. An unoccupied robin's nest was wedged in a forked branch. She could see remnants of blue shell. The leaves were turning from dark green to gold and yellow.

She looked down in time to see Nicolas striding to a work shed. Sunlight undulated over his dark brown hair and the wedge of his shoulders filled out his T-shirt quite nicely.

Hunk alert, she thought, then wondered if she should believe him. Had he never known about Mandy?

He moved like a big cat, lithe and light-footed. When he disappeared from view, Jane left the window and stretched out on the bed. Gazing through the skylight at a patch of blue sky, she kicked off her shoes and reviewed everything he'd said, his every expression, his every gesture. Was he telling her the truth or was he a consummate liar? She couldn't decide—yet. Given a little more time, she knew she'd have a better impression of him, one way or the other.

If he was lying, she'd never forgive him. Lying was something she couldn't tolerate. She'd had too much of it in her life and the lies had scarred her, heart and soul.

Growing up, she'd been told her father's whereabouts were unknown. Then, one day, she'd spied an

envelope in the mailbox from him. After confronting
her mother, she discovered that not only had her
mother known where he was, she had been receiving
child support payments from him. Incensed and feeling betrayed, Jane insisted on contacting him, against
her mother's wishes.

Finally, a phone call had been made, but the result
had been disappointing. No fairy-tale happy endings
for Jane Litton, then or now.

It had taken years before she could trust her mother
again. As for Selena, she'd always been prone to em-
bellishing the truth, expanding on the facts and, well,
lying. But she'd sworn to Jane that Nic had turned his
back on Amanda and he'd known she was pregnant.
Therefore, Selena had never tried to include him in
Mandy's life.

"Was it all a lie?" Jane murmured, then rubbed her
temples where a dull ache persisted.

Having started out at four that morning to find Nic's
house, her energy level ebbed and her eyelids grew
heavy. She dozed and a loincloth-clad Nicolas entered
her dream.

He whispered her name and reached out for her. She
wanted to go to him, but someone held on to her, refusing to release her.

"Traitor!" Selena's voice rasped in her ear. "You're
a traitor, Jane...."

She awoke with a start. Had someone called for her?
She listened and heard Nicolas shout for her again.
Sitting up and shaking the cobwebs from her brain, she
realized he was outside, his voice riding in on a breeze
through the open window. The eyelet curtains danced,

teased by the fragrant air. She sprang from the bed and parted the white curtain. He was standing directly below her window.

"Yes?"

"Were you asleep?"

She patted down her hair. "Uh, I was dozing."

"Sorry to wake you. I'm going up into the tree house and I wanted to let you know in case you went looking for me."

"The what?"

"Tree house." He motioned vaguely to the west. "I've built one over there."

Curiosity won her over. "Will you show me?"

He hesitated, and she knew he was debating whether or not he wanted her company. He probably meant to get away from her. If she had any pride, she'd let him off the hook.

"Please?" She extended a hand, palm out, pride abandoned. "Wait there. I'll be right down."

Not giving him another chance to decline or make excuses, she bounded out of the room, through the house and outside.

"You must have a thing for tree houses," he observed.

"I've never been in one," she confessed. "But I've always wanted to, ever since I was a kid."

"A deprived childhood." He made a *tsking* sound, then gestured for her to follow him. "All right, but be forewarned—I don't allow any strife or arguments or bad feelings up there. It's a place to get away from unpleasant things. So we'll have to put aside our differences for the moment. Agreed?"

She shrugged. "Agreed. I suppose you wanted to be alone and I'm intruding."

"Actually, I'm surprised *you* want *my* company. You've pegged me as a liar and a deadbeat dad, haven't you? Why even want to be around me?"

"I believe in giving everyone the benefit of the doubt. In other words, I'm reserving my judgment. And I thought we were putting all that aside for now."

He glanced back at her. "We are."

Afternoon shadows stretched across the ground, joining deep pockets of shade. She imagined how it would be to live in this wilderness—to awaken to the sound of birdcalls echoing from mountain peak to mountain peak, to sit outside in one of the lawn chairs and sip a cup of morning coffee. Or putter in the garden and fish in the stream, write and paint and photograph in the afternoons and watch dusk settle in the valley pockets from inside the cozy glass house on the bridge. To call this home...what bliss! How could Selena think of this as a bridge to nowhere?

He stopped beside a towering elm that seemed to climb endlessly to the sky. Ladder rungs clung to the massive trunk.

"Ready to make like a monkey?"

She looked up...way up. "I haven't climbed a tree since I was a kid."

"Then you're overdue. Just follow me." He sprang up the ladder like a mountain gorilla.

Shaking her head, Jane climbed the rungs at a sedate pace, testing each one before giving it her weight.

With a sigh of relief, she hoisted herself onto a rectangular platform.

"All I can see are leaves," she noted. The platform was just high enough to be hidden by foliage, no more than ten feet off the ground. "If it were higher, we could see more." She turned in a tight circle and ended up facing him.

He gathered in a deep breath, stretching the cotton T-shirt over his chest. Jane jerked her gaze away from the outline of his flat nipples against the white fabric.

"This is only the first floor. Grab on to me." He didn't wait for her to obey, but placed one of her arms around his waist.

His nearness shot fire through her veins. Jane cautioned her overtaxed heart and tried to wrestle her libido under control. A rope hung between their bodies. She looked up again to see that it disappeared high up into the tree, and that some of the branches had been trimmed to create an unobstructed passage. She glimpsed the bottom of another platform. Nicolas fit one of his feet into the loop at the end of the rope, then kicked a big bag of sand over the side of the stand. With a sudden jolt, she was airborne, feeling like Lois Lane on her first flight with Superman.

Giving a squeak of alarm, she grasped Nicolas more tightly, wrapping her arms around his waist and pressing her cheek to his chest. He laughed, and the sound rumbled in her ear.

"Relax. We're just taking an elevator ride to the sky. We could climb, but this way is quicker and more fun."

He smelled of the forest. Woodsy with a hint of pine. Jane closed her eyes, appreciating the strength emanating from him. Her fingertips discovered the rippling muscles in his broad back and the tautness of his waist. She moved one hand up and the ends of his hair brushed her fingertips. Soft, silky. Like sable. Suddenly, she wanted desperately to run her fingers through it, and that urge brought with it a cold splash of realization. The attraction she'd felt for him back in college was still there—even more so now that she was alone with him in his element.

"Here we are."

Solid planks anchored her feet again. She released him reluctantly, feeling strange, awkward like a teenager. They stood on another platform, this one smaller than the other and affording a view few humans ever saw.

The peaks of the Smokies showed white in the sun and then faded to deep purple. Birds swooped and floated, darting into the trees and then out again. Some of the trees wore autumn colors, others clung to their summer outfits. Evergreens poked through the barrage of bright, flaming hues like stiff fingers of dark green. Gold and yellow, burgundy and red, combined to dazzle the eye. The clouds hung low, creating a gauzy atmosphere. Up here, the air was refined and cooler, meant for loftier species.

Nicolas moved behind her, his body bumping hers. Jane stiffened involuntarily, surprised by the contact and her overreaction. The small platform gave them no choice other than to stand close to each other. He stood behind her and his breath stirred the hair at her temple. An overwhelming, inexplicable peace engulfed her. She wanted to lean her head back and rest it against his shoulder. She knew she was insane to want to nestle against him—this man who might have chosen to ignore his own child—but she also knew he was feeling the magnetic pull, too. She sensed it in his quietness, his stillness. If she looked at him, she knew she would see desire in his eyes. So she didn't look.

Besides, ahead of her paradise beckoned in all its glory—this master work of art called the Great Smokies.

An eagle flew close, so near that Jane could see the deep amber color of his eye. His tail feathers separated like a white fan. Wind whistled under wings that blotted out the sky.

"I wonder if that's the same one," she said, and her voice seemed loud, even though she whispered.

"No, he's banded. The one earlier wasn't. He was young, probably only a year old. That's why I had blood in my eyes."

"Do you have trouble with people shooting them? Where's the thrill in that, anyway?"

"No thrill. It's all for profit."

"I thought eagle feathers have to be registered and can be sold only for religious or spiritual purposes."

"That's right, but for every legitimate market there is a black one with sky-high prices. Two eagles have been killed on my property in the past year. I thought I caught me a poacher today. Standing there with that long branch in your hand...well, rage made my eyes lie to me. I could have sworn you were holding a smoking rifle."

"I didn't get a good look at him. It was all a blur. I wish you had caught him."

"Don't you worry. I will."

A column of smoke smudged the sky, wavering above the treetops. "Is that a fire?" she asked, pointing.

"No, that's from a chimney. Abby's place." His tone was lazy and drawling.

Abby. She'd forgotten about her. Did he share this place with her, too? "It's nice that you have a... companion."

He chuckled, his breath caressing the side of her neck in little puffs. "Companion, huh? Abby would like the sound of that. It would put her in mind of her younger days when she was a real looker and her husband had to fight men off with a stick."

"She's married?"

"Widowed."

"Oh."

"And she's seventy."

She hated herself for the flood of relief that poured through her. This wasn't just a holdover from that silly crush she'd had on him years ago. No, this was sexual fireworks.

"Jane?"

A voice inside told her not to turn toward him, but her heart guided her around to face him. His smile dazzled her. She wanted to kiss him—no!

Did he have any idea how gorgeous he was with the sun spearing his face, lighting his eyes, gliding over his coppery skin?

What was wrong with her? She wasn't usually so...so lustful! But she'd never felt such a strong connection. She could swear she could hear his heart beating in time with hers. He touched the fingertips of one hand to her cheek and his eyes asked her a thousand questions.

Jane placed her hands on his chest. His heart beat quickly beneath his soft cotton T-shirt. Even as she tried to steel herself against her tumult of feelings, her eyelids grew heavy and her lips parted.

He dipped his head. She raised herself on tiptoe. His mouth burned across hers. And then her hands were in his hair, sliding, her nails scraping. And his hands clutched her hair, tugging gently. His tongue swept in, bold and confident. He made a low sound in his throat. One of his hands scorched its way down her spine to her hip.

Something—common sense or complete madness—separated them. Jane stepped back, disengaging herself from his powerful body, his overwhelming allure. She stared into his wide, green eyes, and saw that he was undone, amazed, stunned. Were her brown eyes just as easy to read?

One corner of his mouth quirked, then lifted. He smoothed his hair back with both hands and laughed. "Well, *that* wasn't what either one of us expected."

Her lips throbbed. She wondered if his did, too. "I don't know why I . . . Blame it on an overdose of nature." She turned away from him. "I hope you don't think I do this kind of thing all the time. I didn't come here to—well, you know why I came here."

"To pin my hide to a fence post."

"Yes." She grimaced.

"I hope I didn't offend you. I'm not so lonely that I attack every woman who stumbles into my lair."

She touched her tender lips, aware that she'd never before experienced such profound pleasure from a kiss. *Stop this!* she argued with herself. Stop before it gets completely out of hand.

"Look, let's just drop it. Let's forget it."

"Fine. It's forgotten." He blew out a long breath. "Guess we'd better land. We'll talk more over dinner. I have a lot of questions."

She smiled weakly. "So do I."

He afforded her one more glance before helping her descend from the clouds.

Chapter Four

He liked a woman with a good appetite, Nicolas thought as he watched Jane finish off a third rabbit tamale and her second helping of wild rice and mushroom sauce. He also loved a woman with long legs, tawny blond hair, big, brown bedroom eyes and a mouth made for pleasure giving—and receiving. Tearing his mind from that track, he glanced at her empty plate.

"Want some dessert now?"

"Dessert?" She laid one hand on her flat stomach. "Why didn't you tell me? I would have saved room."

"It's only cookies and coffee."

"Oh, I can handle that." She sat back with a look of satisfaction. "Do you trap all your meat?"

"Yes, and I only kill what I intend to eat. The Cheyenne taught me to use as much of the animal as possible."

"Ah, the Cheyenne." She smiled. "What are you, half and half?"

"Less than half-Cheyenne."

"Less? You sure are more Cheyenne these days than when you were married to Selena."

"How would you know?"

"From what Selena's told me."

"I wouldn't put much stock in her information." As he cleared the table, he harkened back to those distant days when suits and ties were his uniform and he and Selena had struggled with a marriage that should have ended as a brief but thrilling affair. "Sometimes it takes years before you find your true self," he commented, lost in the memories before snapping back to the present. Jane was frowning at him, probably because of what he'd said about her sister. "Go on into the living room. I'll bring the coffee tray."

He went into the kitchen and arranged the coffee service and plate of lemon cooler cookies on a tray. He wondered if Jane was as confused about him as he was about her. His thoughts skipped like a stone across rippling water—that kiss...the accusations she'd hurled at him about being uncaring, selfish...a child, *his* daughter.

He carried the rattan tray into the living room and set it on the low coffee table. Jane sat on the couch. Her expression was more guarded now, less friendly. Time to talk, he thought. Time to put on the boxing gloves.

"What do you take in your coffee?"

"A little cream, please." She sat forward to accept the cup and saucer. "You bought this land while you were still married, didn't you?"

"Yes. I got it in the settlement. Selena came away with the houses in Dallas and Los Angeles, as you know. I finished building this after the divorce."

"Where did you live while you were having it built?"

"I didn't *have* it built. *I* built it. And I lived in a tent and then a tepee."

She raised her brows. "Even in the winter?"

He nodded. "Tepees are warm, if you erect them correctly."

She blew at the steam rising from the cup. "What did you mean about taking a while before knowing your true self?"

He settled back in his favorite easy chair. "I feel more comfortable now than ever before. I used to be things for other people—a good student, a dedicated protégé, a powerful businessman—but this is the first time in my life where I'm comfortable with who I am."

She sipped the coffee. "Who are you?"

He regarded her, wary of her question and her motive. "I'm a conservationist, an environmentalist, a Cheyenne, a man of honor."

"And a father." She set the cup and saucer on the table. "Or do you still doubt that?"

"I have some doubts and a hundred questions, but I don't think you'll have the answers."

"Ask away." She sat back and linked her hands around one knee. "*I'm* not into hiding or shying away from the truth."

He decided he'd shatter her smugness. "Okay. When did this pregnancy happen? Selena and I made love two or three times those last few months, at most, so when was it? The last time? That night I was half-sloshed and Selena accused me of flirting with another woman, and then in the next breath tried to get me into the sack because she believed a child would solve all our problems?"

Irritation and uneasiness flashed in her eyes. "Okay, okay, so I can't answer *all* your questions, but I could answer a *few*—reasonable ones."

"If this is true, I should be talking to your sister, not to you."

"Selena would hit the ceiling if she knew I was here."

"If I decide this child might be mine, she'll hear from me whether she likes it or not."

"I didn't come here to make trouble."

He leaned his elbows on his knees, edging closer to her. "Why *did* you come here, Jane?"

She didn't meet his gaze. "I told you. I thought it was time you acknowledged your daughter."

"But why now, after six years?"

She stood and moved to stare out the windows. "Seemed like the time was right," she answered vaguely. "Mandy would love this place. Too bad she's never gotten to see it."

"That's not my fault," he asserted.

She shot him a glare. "Why would Selena lie?"

"Why, indeed?" he challenged. "Unless, of course, the child isn't mine."

"She's yours," she said with unfailing certainty. "You might as well accept it. You're a daddy. Is that so horrible? I just don't understand men like you." She hugged herself tightly, her back ramrod straight. He could see her reflection in the window and her expression was tense, haunted. There was more to this than she was admitting, but she wasn't willing to reveal it. He decided to prod her.

"Men like me? You've known men like me, huh? Tell me about it, Jane."

She sighed, glanced furtively at him, then gave a quick, defensive shrug. "My dad never had anything to do with me, either, and let me tell you something, pal, it hurts."

Nicolas sipped his coffee and waited, giving her time to pry the words out of her heart. This was personal, as he'd suspected. The lady had been betrayed, bruised, and she didn't want the same things to happen to her niece.

She blinked rapidly. "I spent my whole childhood wondering why I wasn't worthy of his love—how he could turn his back on me and never even send me a cheap, little birthday card. I don't want Amanda to go through that."

He emptied his coffee cup, mulling over her confession and wondering if she knew she'd revealed a big chunk of her emotional makeup to him.

"I'm puzzled," he confessed. "If you thought I was such a rotter, why try to drag me into your niece's life? Wouldn't she be better off without me?"

"I didn't know if you were a rotter or not."

"Then you didn't believe Selena."

"I didn't . . . people change."

"Giving me the benefit of the doubt again?" He smiled and was glad when she smiled back. "Selena said I knew about my child and chose to ignore her. What does that make me, if not a self-centered bastard?"

"It makes you one of the many foolish men in this country who divorce the wife *and* the children and never look back." She turned to face him. "People have all kinds of reasons for doing what they do. I wanted to hear yours."

"I have a hell of a reason. I didn't know I was a father."

"And you didn't want to be a father when you were married to Selena."

"That's right."

"Aside from your marriage being shaky, was there any other reason for your not wanting a child?"

He leaned back in the chair, wondering if he should get into this with her. Sensing a compassionate soul, he decided to go ahead and open that can of worms.

"My brother was another reason."

"Where is he? You said he visited, so I take it he doesn't live here with you."

"No." He fashioned a grim smile. "He's in the navy, as a matter-of-fact."

"Really?" She sat down again and crossed her long legs. "Didn't you have custody of him after your parents died in that car wreck?"

"That's right, but I can't take any credit for how Rich turned out. My uncle took him under his wing."

"But he lived with you and Selena for a while."

"Yes, but not for long." He sighed, feeling weighted by the memories. Stupid of him to bring all this up again. Should have kept the memories in that can, tightly shut. He poured himself another cup of coffee, sensing her watchfulness and realizing he would have to tell her something. "My business was in full swing and I couldn't—*didn't* give Richie the time he needed. My uncle took over."

"How old was Rich then?"

"Thirteen."

She pursed her lips and glanced up as if for divine guidance. "That's a tough age. I gave my mother fits when I was thirteen."

Her understanding of that prickly stage of adolescence loosened the knot tightening in his stomach. "Lucky for both me and Richie, Uncle Vern is a great father. He'd raised four sons before he took Rich in."

"I take it you found Rich to be a handful."

Nicolas stirred sugar into his coffee. He wondered if she knew this history and if she was testing him to see if he'd tell the truth. He gave a mental shrug. He had nothing to hide, despite her assessment of him.

"Richie rebelled after my parents died. He needed someone to sit on him and straighten him out, but I was busy being the wonder boy of the business world. He ended up in juvenile detention for stealing a car, then he ran away and was missing for two months before he was picked up in San Francisco."

"You must have been frantic!" Her brown eyes widened.

Yes, you should have been, you sorry excuse for a brother, a dark voice in his mind taunted.

"Like I said, I was busy." He shook his head, refusing to cut himself some slack, refusing to fall back on that same old song so many absentee dads hummed. "I was self-centered and irritated with my brother for taking up any of my precious time. I hired a detective to track him down, but I didn't waste much time worrying about him."

He winced, hating who he used to be. "When he was finally located, Uncle Vern went to pick him up at the police station and took him home with him. Richie came by a week later and packed up his things. I never said anything to him about moving in with Uncle Vern." He laughed, bitterness welling in his throat and shame tying knots in his stomach. God, he'd been such a self-serving, egotistical fool back then! "I was just glad he was gone and I could get on with my life, uninterrupted."

Jane propped her feet on the edge of the coffee table. "Sounds like you were in the 'me' stage."

He tilted his head to one side, thinking he'd heard her wrong. "Say what?"

"It's my life theory," she explained, gesturing with her long-fingered hands. "First you have the 'mother' stage where your primary care giver is your whole world, then you go through your 'us' stage where you try to belong, try to be in the 'in' crowd and be popular." She took a breath and pink colored her cheeks. "Shall I go on?"

"Don't stop now," he teased, thinking she was cute when she was a little embarrassed.

"Okay, where was I? Oh, right. Next is the 'me' stage from about age eighteen and on into your twenties when you concentrate on yourself—what you want, what you need, where you're going with your career. It's bad to get married or have children during that stage."

"What's the next stage?"

"The 'we' stage. Marriage. You want to couple. You're ready to share, to build something together, to commit."

He smiled, admiring the thought she'd put behind her theory. "And next?"

"The 'seed' stage when you concentrate on your kids, if you have them. If you don't, you usually find something to nurture—nephews, nieces, dogs, cats...."

"I missed that one, I guess."

She glanced around, a smile spreading across her lips. "I don't think so. This house has been your baby. And you still have many, many years of the 'seed' period left. When you reach your fifties or sixties, you enter your 'we-me' stage. It's a time when your focus returns to the couple unit or the single unit. If you have a long life, you eventually return to the 'mother' stage."

"Really? Isn't Mother dead by then?"

She laughed. "Yes, but you end up with a care giver, who generally becomes your world."

He nodded, grasping her wisdom. "Nursing homes, hospitals, retirement homes. So your theory has us coming full circle."

"Fitting, huh?"

"Very, and impressive. You've obviously given this a lot of thought." He studied his surroundings, recalling the care he'd taken in choosing everything. "So this is my baby. Well, it *has* been a labor of love."

"That's obvious."

"What about Selena? Is she a good mother?"

Jane crossed her arms and ankles. "She worships Mandy. We all do."

"We?"

"Mother and our other relatives. When Mandy was a baby we passed her around like she was a Kewpie doll." She laughed lightly. "She should be an insufferable, spoiled brat, but she's not. She's a sweetheart."

Resentment sprang up in him, slicing and telling. So they'd all had a good time raising his child. Was that supposed to make him happy?

Nicolas finished his second cup of coffee so quickly he burned his mouth. It left a bitter aftertaste, which suited his mood.

"Why are you frowning?" she asked.

"Because I'm a tad resentful that everyone had such a swell time with my daughter."

"So you believe that she *is* your daughter?"

"I'm assuming as much for the time being. I think you believe it to be true."

"Well, that's a beginning, I suppose." Yawning, she placed a hand to her mouth. "Sorry, it's been a long day."

She looked dead tired. Nicolas assessed the situation and decided that she wasn't in any condition to sit up most of the night answering his thousand and one questions.

"Why don't you stay one extra day?"

"Are you sure you can stand the company? I thought you wanted to get rid of me as quickly as possible."

"I changed my mind."

"What changed it?"

He grinned, giving in to his devilish streak. "That encounter in the tree house."

The sound of her teeth clicking together and the widening of her expressive eyes made him want to laugh, but he smothered it. No use rubbing salt in the wound.

"That—I thought we were going to forget that."

"It's hard to forget." Seeing how uncomfortable he'd made her, he relented. "You're tired and I need some time to think. I suggest that you go to bed and we'll talk tomorrow. If this child is mine, I want to know about her and I want to know why you waited six years to tell me about her." He held up one hand. "But we can sort through all this tomorrow, if you agree to stay an extra day."

She nodded. "Sounds like a good plan."

"Great. Need me to show you the way to your room again?"

"No, I left a bread crumb trail." She smiled and extended one slender hand. "'Night, Nic. I'm glad we're not screaming at each other anymore."

He stood and shook her hand. "So am I. Sleep well."

"Oh, I will." She moved toward the doorway. "I'll be out like a light, I'm sure. It's this country air."

He listened to her footsteps grow faint and the door to her bedroom close before he picked up the tray and took it into the kitchen.

Anger for his ex-wife built steadily within him. They'd hurt each other before and during the divorce, but had managed to leave each other alone after the marriage ended. Until now.

He leaned his hot face against the cool exterior of the refrigerator and told himself that the anger boiling inside him wasn't good. He wanted to be an adult about this. But he also wanted to shout and kick and curse Selena.

Whether he liked it or not, he would have to contact his ex-wife and open old wounds. Damn her. If she'd kept his own daughter from him... He backed off that thought and the fury that rose within him along with it.

He had a feeling this could get ugly, and he dreaded it. The peace he'd fought so hard to find in these dense woods was gone, plucked from him by Selena's leggy half-sister.

THE NEXT MORNING they hiked to Jane's rented car and she drove them into Asheville where Nic said he needed to pick up some supplies. During the drive she'd told him incidental things about Mandy—where she went to school, what her interests were, her favorite movies, the ballet recital last month when she had been center stage, a ham, just like her mother.

She parked in the grocery-store lot and Nic pulled a list from his shirt pocket. He looked crisp in chinos and a madras shirt, despite the morning hike to the car.

"Don't let me forget the rock salt. I want to churn some ice cream."

"Check," she said. "But only if I get a taste."

"Done. I'll get the groceries first, then I've got to pop into that drugstore next door and buy some vitamins and cold medicine."

She sent him a curious glance.

"Winter's coming and I believe in being prepared."

Jane nodded, approving of his plan. She went inside the grocery store with him and was surprised when a cashier and a stock boy immediately called greetings to him.

"Hey, there, Alice! I thought you only worked on weekends," Nic responded to the cashier.

"Lucy had her baby, so I'm taking her shift," the red-haired woman answered.

"She had her baby? What was it?"

"A girl," the sack boy responded with a toothy grin. "They named her Anastasia Elizabeth. Isn't that a mouthful?"

Nicolas chuckled. "Yes, but it's pretty. I'll have to get her a gift. What do you think she needs, Alice?"

"Besides a full-time nanny?" Alice wisecracked. "Say, they've got vaporizers on sale next door at the drugstore. You always need those come winter."

"Good idea. Thanks."

He didn't introduce Jane, so she was reduced to smiling and acting as if she fit in—which she didn't. She wandered toward the junk food section and grabbed sweet rolls and candy bars, a sure sign that she was nervous or depressed. Nervous, she decided. She had nothing to be depressed about since it seemed that Nicolas might not have known he was a father. But would he do anything about it? Would he want to have a relationship with his daughter? Or did he continue to believe he wasn't good father material? If she kept this up, she *would* be depressed.

And then there was Selena. Once she found out about this little trip, life would get even rougher. But she shouldn't dwell on that now, Jane thought. Plenty of time later to deal with Selena's rage. She had lots of experience with that. Her sister was notorious for her temper tantrums, being the ultimate prima donna.

She heard other people greet Nicolas warmly and she realized she'd have to further alter her previous perception of him. Assuming he was a hermit, she'd pictured him alone in his house in the woods, never seeing anyone, going into town only when it was absolutely necessary and then having nothing to do with anyone. Scratch that, she thought with a wry smile. The man was a social animal.

At least six people had already spoken to him, and she'd heard two ask him to dinner. He'd been living a well-rounded life. She wondered if he had a girlfriend stashed somewhere in Asheville.

After paying for the groceries and stowing them in the car, Nic went to the drugstore while Jane bought two sacks of ice, which she put in an insulated chest. How were they going to cart all of this back to the house? she wondered. She counted the bags in the trunk—four, plus the sack of rock salt and the ice chest.

When she entered the drugstore she found him at the front counter, paying for vitamins, cold medicine, a vaporizer and a card for the new baby. The irony set her teeth on edge. Buying a present for another woman's child while his own went fatherless.

The clerk tried to engage him in gossip about the town, but he didn't seem interested. When the clerk cracked a joke and earned a laugh from him, Jane saw Mandy in his smile. He paid for his items and headed out the door. Jane had to trot to catch up with him.

"Where's the fire, chief?" she asked. "Remember me? Or have I suddenly become invisible?"

He pulled a piece of paper from the bag and held it in front of her face.

"What's this?"

"Read it and weep."

She snatched the paper from his fingers and stared at the message from his ex-wife.

"I sent her a fax while I was in the drugstore. I asked her if Amanda is mine and she fired this one back at me."

The words seemed to smoke on the white page: *Don't ever contact me again or you'll hear from my attorney. Selena.*

Jane groaned and handed the paper back to him. Her stomach dropped to her feet.

"She's still the same sweet girl I remember," he said, his tone dripping with insincerity.

"Why didn't you discuss this with me first?" Jane demanded. "You've placed me in a terrible position."

"No, you did that to yourself, and besides, I didn't mention your name."

"But Selena isn't stupid. She'll figure out that I looked you up."

"I don't know about that, but I *do* know one thing for sure now."

"What?"

"Amanda's mine."

Chapter Five

"Hey, there, neighbor!"

Jane and Nic turned to inspect the white-haired woman with bright blue eyes. She joined them and Nic embraced her.

"Hi, there, neighbor." He plucked the fax from Jane's hand, folded it neatly and slid it into the back pocket of his chinos. He sent her a warning frown before smiling benignly at the other woman. "Did you hear about Lucy's baby?"

"Yes, I just heard." The woman glanced at Jane again, then held out her hand. "Well, since Nic has forgotten his manners, I'll introduce myself. I'm Abby Masters, his nearest neighbor."

"Hello. I'm Jane Litton." Jane examined the woman's friendly face and kind eyes. So this was Abby. "Nic has already told me about you. I'm...visiting. Nic and I used to be in-laws."

"Really?" Abby raised her brows, clearly intrigued. "How long will you be visiting?" .

"I'm leaving tomorrow." She looked at Nicolas, who refused to meet her gaze.

"Abby, someone shot at an eagle yesterday on my land. Jane witnessed it, but she didn't get a good look at the shooter."

"Oh, too bad." Abby drew her snowy eyebrows together. "I wish we could find one of those guys and have him jailed. You feel that nip in the air, Nic? Winter is on the way. I'm hoarding firewood like a squirrel hoards nuts."

"I'll bring you a rick," Nic promised.

"Will you?" Abby's attention was diverted by an ice cream truck, its song floating across the lot. "Anybody for a frozen yogurt?"

"Jane said she wanted ice cream earlier," Nic volunteered, giving her a slight push. "You go ahead. I'll load this stuff into the car."

"You don't want one?" Abby asked.

"No, but you two have one on me." He pressed a bill into Abby's palm and winked.

"Why, isn't that sweet of you!" Abby waved down the ice cream truck.

"The car's locked. Here, the keys are in my purse." Jane started to hand over her leather clutch, then pulled back. "You won't drive off and leave me here, will you?" she asked, only half kidding. He was in a weird mood.

"Don't be ridiculous." He took the purse from her and went to the car while Jane joined Abby at the ice cream truck.

The driver was a teenage boy with an outbreak of acne and a mouthful of braces.

"I want a banana frozen yogurt," Abby said. "What's your pleasure, Jane?"

"Oh, let's see." She scanned the pictures of offerings pasted to the side of the truck. "That rainbow ice cream looks good to me."

"A banana and a rainbow," the boy repeated. "Cup or cone?"

"Cup," Abby and Jane chorused.

Jane smiled. "Great minds think alike."

Abby laughed good-naturedly. "Nicolas doesn't get many visitors. In fact, he pretty much keeps to himself."

"He didn't actually invite me. I kind of showed up," Jane admitted with a shrug.

"Here you go, ladies. That'll be two and a half, please."

Abby handed him Nic's five. "I remember when a little cup of cream like this cost a nickel. Of course, I also remember when television was invented." Abby chuckled, her blue eyes dancing. "Wasn't it nice of Nicolas to treat us?"

"Yes." Jane slipped a spoonful of the frozen cream into her mouth and twisted around to look at the car. Nic had finished putting the purchases in the trunk and was sitting in the passenger seat, waiting for her. His head was bent, and she thought he was probably studying Selena's response again. That fax had started World War III. Jane shut her eyes for a moment, dreading her next confrontation with her explosive sister.

"Tastes good, doesn't it?" Abby asked.

"Oh, yes. Delicious."

"I've got to finish my shopping." Abby extended the change from the five dollars. "Will you give this to Nicolas and thank him again for me?"

"Sure." Jane took the money. "I'm glad I got to meet you. Nic speaks fondly of you."

"He's been like a son to me. It's nice that you two are still friendly after the divorce. That doesn't happen often. Divorces usually turn people into verbal snipers."

Jane could see why Nicolas would like this woman. Dressed in walking shorts and a flowered, sleeveless shirt, Abby's face shone with good humor. She was tanned and fit, her legs looking as if they belonged to a forty-year-old instead of a seventy-year-old. Her wide-brimmed straw hat hung from a chin strap. She pulled it up, covering her short white hair and shading her face.

Deciding she should be silent on the subject of Nicolas and her family, Jane extended her free hand.

"Goodbye."

"Goodbye, dear. Maybe I'll see you again."

Jane shrugged. "You never know. It's a small world."

Walking back to the car, she opened the door and slid in behind the wheel. She glanced at Nic, then did a double take when she saw he was holding her wallet open to the picture section.

"Well, help yourself to my stuff, Thunderheart," she drawled, but her sarcasm dissipated when she noted the taut set of his mouth and the shadows under his eyes. He was looking at Mandy's picture.

"I wanted to see," he said, his voice raw around the edges.

"You could have asked first." She had two photos of Amanda in her wallet—a studio shot and a Polaroid she'd taken of Mandy at the zoo kissing a llama. Both pictures were adorable, both revealed what Jane knew had placed that tight expression of shock on Nicolas's face. He had seen his daughter's eyes, her coloring, dark brown hair—all inherited from her father, Nicolas Thunderheart.

"I would have shown you the photographs." She grabbed his hand and pushed the change into it. "Thanks for the ice cream. Abby's nice. I like her."

He stuffed the money into his shirt pocket, then turned to stare out the side window. He propped his chin in his hand, his long fingers covering the lower half of his face. Jane saw the shimmer of tears in his eyes. He was undone, she knew, so she gave him whatever privacy she could afford in the confines of the car.

She started the engine and headed in the direction of his place. He stared gloomily at the passing blur of scenery. Jane wished she were a mind reader. She could feel his pain, but what else? She knew how she'd feel— she'd feel like murdering Selena.

The turnoff to his land loomed up ahead. Jane crushed the empty ice cream cup in her hand and dropped it into the litter bag dangling from the car's radio knob. She slowed the sedan and took the turn. The bumpy road dead-ended a mile into the brush. She braked and looked at him. He still hadn't moved.

"Well?" Jane said, uncertainty making her voice quiver a little. She turned off the engine. "Looks like the end of the trail for us."

He straightened in the seat and looked around as if coming out of a trance. It hurt Jane to see the look of betrayal and frustration lingering on his face, in his eyes. She wanted to open her arms to him, but she suspected he wouldn't welcome the gesture.

"I'm sorry that Selena was so blunt and threatening in her fax."

"If she hadn't been, I wouldn't have believed your story about Amanda. When Selena goes on the defensive, she's lying or hiding something."

Jane quirked her brows, impressed. He certainly had Selena's number. "I understand what you must be feeling—"

"You have no idea," he interrupted, finally swinging his gaze around to her. "She's mine." The possessiveness in his voice startled her. "Selena had our child and hid her from me. Why? *I want to know why!* His voice shook with anger, then he wrenched open the door and flung himself out of the compact car.

Jane stared, slack jawed, as he tore through the woods. Only after he'd disappeared from view did an alarm bell ring in her numb brain. She scrambled from the car.

"Hey!" she called in the direction he'd gone. "Where do you think you're going? Don't leave me out here. I don't know where—" He reappeared, thrashing through the brush, dragging a crudely fashioned travois behind him.

Delivering a black look, he strode past her. "Open the trunk," he ordered.

She obeyed with a surly expression stamped on her face, resenting that he was taking out on her what her sister deserved. "I've been wondering how we were going to carry all these things through the woods. You're strong, but you'd still need a couple of extra arms." She eyed the two long poles and the skins stretched between them. "Did you make this?"

"Yes."

"You keep it hidden somewhere nearby?"

"Yes." He piled their purchases onto the stretcher.

She propped her hands on her hips. Her irritation with his attitude flared. "Why didn't you discuss it with me before you sent Selena that fax? And how did you know where to send it?"

"I've kept up with her. We still have some financial links, you know."

"Did it occur to you that you've placed me in a bad situation? I told you that Selena didn't know anything about me being here or telling you about Amanda. She probably won't even speak to me again."

"My heart bleeds for you."

She wanted to kick him, but she doubled up her fist and punched him in the arm instead. He was so solid, the punch damaged her far more than it did him. He regarded her with a mixture of curiosity, impatience and amusement.

"Ow." She rubbed her stinging knuckles, then sucked the middle one. "You hurt me."

He let loose a scoffing laugh. *"Excuse me? I* hurt *you?"*

"Yes." She saw that the car trunk had been emptied, so she slammed the lid shut.

"Forgive me for getting in the way of your fist," he drawled.

"I've tried to be big about this, you know. I didn't have to come here and let you know about Amanda. You should be thanking me instead of throwing sarcasm in my face."

He whirled around to confront her. "Thank you for tracking me down and accusing me of being a deadbeat dad, of being a louse, of being lower than dirt. I owe you a huge debt of gratitude." He leaned into her, his snarling mouth blurring before her eyes. "Thanks loads, sweetheart."

Infuriated, Jane planted a hand against his shoulder and used all her strength to shove him aside. "You'd better be nice to me if you want me to stay and answer your questions. I don't have to, you know."

"No, but you will." He smirked as she fumed at him. "You don't want to leave."

"Says who?"

"Says anybody who knows anything about you." He grabbed the ends of the poles and took long strides toward the dense forest. Jane fell into step behind him, carting her purse and a sack from the drugstore. "You want to know what makes me tick to see if I'm worthy enough to be around Amanda."

She resented him being right and threw daggers at his back with her eyes. "You've probably ruined everything by faxing Selena before I could talk to her."

"I'm not afraid of Selena."

"Well, you ought to be! She'll decide whether you'll see Mandy or not."

"I think a judge would disagree."

"A judge?" She hurried to catch up and overtake him. Making a grab for him, she snagged his shirt-sleeve. "Hold up. You're not thinking about suing for custody, are you? Because, if you are, then you're being selfish and not giving Mandy any consideration."

"Why shouldn't I? I have a six-year-old daughter who thinks I deserted her!"

"No, she doesn't."

"She doesn't?" He narrowed his eyes. "What *does* she think about me?"

Jane winced, hating to have to say it. "She thinks you're dead."

He actually staggered backward before he caught himself and stood as straight and imposing as a palace guard. "That," he said in a chilling voice, "I will never forgive. Never." Then he started off again, dragging the travois, his long legs eating up the uneven ground.

Jane could only follow, her steps less certain, her breath rasping in her throat, her heart heavy with its burden. She'd never agreed with Selena about telling Mandy that her father was dead. They'd had many arguments about it, but Selena was Mandy's mother and her will prevailed. But now Jane was taking the brunt of that awful lie.

She didn't think things could get any worse until they reached the house . . . and saw the bear.

"WHAT'S HE DOING?" Jane asked from her crouched position behind Nicolas.

"Looking for food, I guess. Bears are eating everything in sight now, getting ready for hibernation." He shifted to get a better view of the black bear, which was sniffing around the small smokehouse. "I can't let him get in there," Nicolas said, mostly to himself. "There isn't much inside, but what I've got, I want to keep."

"Are you going to shoot him?"

He looked back at her, noting the fright in her eyes and the clutch of her hands on his shoulders. "What am I supposed to shoot him with, a murderous glare?"

She gave him a quick once-over. "You mean, you aren't carrying a weapon?"

"I have a buck knife in my pocket, but I doubt that would do much good against a full-grown bear."

"I thought you mountain men always carried rifles."

"Us mountain men, huh?" He chuckled. The woman could be insufferably cute, he thought. The bear pounded on the smokehouse door, forcing him to form a plan of action. His best weapon was surprise, making the first move and bluffing the animal. "You stay put," he cautioned Jane, although he didn't think the order was necessary. She seemed to have taken root.

"Wh-what are you going to do?"

"Play chicken."

He took a deep breath and charged from the underbrush, arms stretched wide, a fearsome expression on his face, legs pumping. He emitted a horrific growl that swung the bear around to him.

"Are you nuts?" Jane whispered at his back, but he ignored her and snarled at the furry trespasser.

The bear rose on its hind legs and sized him up. Swaying from side to side, it fashioned a growl of its own, and Nicolas had to admit that the animal's was deeper and more dangerous sounding. Waving its big front claws, the bear peeled back its lips to display impressive teeth.

An arrow of apprehension pierced Nic's bravado and he pulled his knife from his back pocket and flicked it open, just in case. Maybe he could go for the eyes or snout if there was an attack.

The intruder stilled and Nic could have sworn he saw its eyes narrow. The hair stood up on the back of his neck. It was going to charge him!

Then his peripheral vision picked up a flash of white, blue and yellow scuttle past, roll on the grass and come to rest near the beast.

The animal sniffed, gathered up the plastic-wrapped item in one claw, tore it open, gave another sniff and resumed its swaying motion.

Nic glanced back over his shoulder. "What the hell was that?" he whispered.

"A bag of honey-nut rolls," Jane responded, her voice shaking, breathless.

The bear stuffed the bag of goodies into its mouth and settled on all fours. Dismissing Nicolas completely, the animal lumbered away from the house and toward the cool shadows of the dense forest. Only when its gleaming black coat could no longer be seen among the tree trunks and green-and-gold undergrowth did Nicolas release his breath. He folded the knife and stuck it back into his pocket.

"Hey, it worked." Jane bounded from the brush, clearly full of herself and in high spirits from coming to his rescue so successfully. "I'm sure glad I gave in to temptation and bought those rolls at the grocery bakery." She scrutinized him, a self-assured grin on her lips. "You okay, Tarzan?"

He felt one side of his mouth quirk, although he wasn't in a good humor. Oh, she thought she was so clever, so cheeky. She was cruisin'.... "Yes, Cheetah."

"No, no." She tapped a forefinger against the third button on his shirt placket. "Jane. The name is Jane, Tarzan. Just like in the book and the movies. That old bear rattled your brain pan, didn't it? When you can't tell a woman from a chimp..." Her winged-shaped eyebrows arched. "My, my, it *has* been a long time, hasn't it, Nickie? You need to get out of these woods more often and scrounge up some female company. You know what they say, use it or lo—"

That did it. He silenced her sassy mouth by wrapping an arm around her waist and his lips around hers. When he pulled away from her, he laughed at her shocked expression.

"What are you doing?" she asked, sputtering.

"Keeping in practice. I'm taking your advice. Use it or lose it, right?" He stamped her mouth with another kiss, but then got tangled in her web of sexuality.

Longing bubbled up in him like some pocket of trapped passion suddenly released. He forgot that Jane was trouble, that she'd consorted with the devil to keep his child from him. All he remembered was that her lips were incredibly soft and her body fit his like the missing piece of a puzzle. Her lips parted and his tongue slid home. Her fingers tugged at the ends of his hair, then spread over his shoulders. She slanted her mouth more completely beneath his and Nic stroked her, teased her, until he elicited her soft whimpers of pleasure. He slipped his hands down to cup her buttocks. She was firm, rounded, perfect. She was all any man would want. And he wanted.

"Nic...Nic..." Her voice penetrated his woolly brain. "Stop this." She wiggled from his embrace and beat a hasty retreat from his arms. Patting down wispy strands of her blond hair, she pursed her glistening lips and blew out a long breath. "You don't need any more practice. You're way ahead of most of the Casanovas I've known, but we can't let ourselves get carried away."

He nodded, aching and longing for more of her. Her skin was flushed and her eyes were full of sparkles. She moistened her lips with the tip of her tongue, and fire licked at his loins. Skirting around the heart of the issue seemed pointless. He wasn't the kind of man to pretend he didn't feel things when he did.

"What I know is that we have something going on between us," he said, and as he expected, she looked cornered. She could no more turn off her emotions than he could.

"I didn't come here to play lip-lock with you. I'm here for Amanda, remember?"

"Oh, yes." His passion cooled, but only slightly. "And I won't ever be forgetting her now that I know she exists." All the hurt came crashing down on him again. "How could you allow Selena to keep this from me? How could you tell my own daughter I'm dead?"

She stared at him, her mouth opening and closing, but giving him no answers.

He strode away, his anger renewed and stronger than ever. And the pain was wicked—that stabbing pain of betrayal. He heard her following him. "When I think of what you've done, I . . . well, you're lucky I'm *not* a wild mountain man or *you'd* be the one nailed to a post."

"I didn't cause this mess. I'm the one who is trying to straighten it out."

He started to unlock the front door, but he stopped. Facing her again, he pointed a finger at her nose. "No. You came here to call me on the carpet and do a dance on me. Don't try to pretty it up and make it sound as if you're some kind of avenging angel. You're not."

"Get your finger out of my face before I bite it in two." She batted aside his hand. "And make up your mind. Are we going to be enemies or friends? I can't stand this kiss and cuss mentality."

He glared at her, torn between wanting to kiss her again and call her every vile name he could think of.

"Nicolas, are we going to work together on this Amanda problem or are you going to force me to fight against you? Remember, I'm here for my niece. I want what is best for her." She narrowed her eyes, challenging him. "So tell me true, Nicolas Thunderheart. Friends or foes?"

Curse her brown eyes! He looked away from her for a moment in quiet surrender. "Friends, damn it." Turning aside, he shoved the key in the lock and opened the door. "Come on inside and we'll plot our strategy."

Chapter Six

Staring into the flickering flames of the camp fire, Nic gave a long sigh, tugging at Jane's heartstrings. She sat near him, the camp fire he'd built chasing away the night's chill. She wondered what he was thinking as the silence began to take on weight.

They'd managed to keep the conversation light and friendly while putting away the groceries, planning the evening meal and cooking it. Their dinner discussion had been pleasant, safe. No mention of Selena or Mandy. But it was coming. Like the dawn, it was inevitable.

In the flickering light of the fire, with shadows cavorting over his face, he seemed proud and impervious, like a lion reigning over his territory and minding his pride—although this lion's pride consisted only of himself and a cub he'd never seen. Yes, she felt sorry for him and guilty for thinking the worst of him.

Her attention shifted to his hands as he pitched twigs into the flames. His fingers were long and blunt ended—and magical, she thought, her skin tingling as she recalled the tender-rough caresses, the knowing strokes and pats. When those hands were on her, she became all instinct.

It was kind of like going native, she cracked wise with herself, smiling at the peculiar behavior he evoked in her. She couldn't truthfully say she didn't like the way he made her feel—it was exhilarating to flirt with the idea of giving over to her basic instincts and forgetting all the trappings of morals and decorum. Exhilarating and dangerous. She could get hurt. Seriously hurt. Because, as a woman, she would end up giving him everything—her heart, her soul, her love. And that might be more than he'd want.

"What's her last name?" he asked without warning.

Jane braced herself. Now that he'd taken his finger from the dike, a flood of questions was sure to follow. "Mandy, you mean? Carr. Her last name is Carr."

"Selena's maiden name. I'm listed as 'father' on the birth certificate, but she doesn't even let my child use my last name?"

"You know, Nic, before I came here and met you, I could justify most of what Selena did. I can't now. But she always insisted you knew about the pregnancy, but that you never even called to ask if the baby was a boy or girl. Under those circumstances, I thought Selena had every right not to hang your last name on the child you didn't want." Jane picked up a bit of a twig and tossed it into the fire. "I'm having a hard time understanding why she has done all of this. You must have left her with a clear impression that you wanted nothing to do with children—ever."

"And what if I did? Does that give her the right to never tell me she was pregnant, that she had our child?" He stretched out on his side and cradled his head in one hand. "Look, during that time I was a mess. My business was going under, my reputation was shot to hell, I was still feeling guilty for not being able to give my brother what he needed, and my marriage was on its last legs. Any discussion of having kids during that time was met with an emphatic 'Hell, no!' But can you blame me?"

"No, I suppose not." Jane slanted him a look, wondering if he'd talk about the business scandal. She wanted to know why he'd been so dense when he was supposed to be so smart. "What happened to your business, Nic? How'd you get caught fraternizing with the enemy?"

"I listened to the wrong people." He frowned, then looked up to pin her with an astute gaze. "Like someone else I know. So how much do you know about what happened back then?"

Pulling her knees up to her chest, Jane warded off the chill of guilt. Maybe she had believed Selena's stories about him being a deadbeat dad, but she had not believed all the horrible tales she'd read about him. "Only what I read in the papers, saw on television."

"Then you don't know anything," he said, bitterly.

"The media reported that you'd built your business advising clients to invest in companies that didn't pollute the environment. But you were caught heavily investing your clients' money in a shipping firm that dumped medical waste and in which you were a stockholder yourself. You and your pal, Barrett Prescott, were majority stockholders, I believe.''

She remembered her shock, her quick denial, when she'd read the accounts. But the reports of unscrupulous behavior continued until she had wrestled with a sliver of doubt. She'd refused to believe that she'd been horribly duped. Something else had happened, something the media hadn't reported.

''I was crushed when I read about it,'' she admitted. ''It broke my heart when they called you a fat-cat hypocrite.''

''You're like everybody else, aren't you?''

She bristled. ''What's that mean?''

''That means that you believe every bad thing you read and don't bother to wait for the facts to come out.''

''I didn't say I believed it all.'' She grabbed at a kernel of enlightenment in his statement. ''What facts?''

''If you had bothered to look beyond the headlines, you would know what I'm talking about.''

''What was I supposed to see behind the headlines?''

''A man who had trusted too much, but who had learned a valuable lesson. I invested my trust in the wrong people, but I'll never make that mistake again.''

She cringed. ''I didn't want to believe the worst about you.''

''Yes, you did. And so did Selena.'' He barked a harsh laugh. ''When it all came down on me like a hailstorm, Selena said I deserved it and she wasn't sinking with me. She packed her bags and left me.

Guess she never heard that one about standing by her man."

Jane winced, wanting to come to her sister's defense, but finding it impossible after hearing his side of the story. "Selena said you asked her to leave."

His smile was so sad it hurt to witness it. "I told her that if she thought I was a crook, then she should clear out. I suppose one could interpret that as asking her to leave."

Jane picked up a stick and used it to draw a question mark in the dirt. "Like they say, there are two sides to every story." And which was she supposed to believe? Had Selena lied about everything? Nic didn't seem to be lying. Maybe the truth was somewhere in between their accounts of what happened back then.

"What stage are *you* in?"

She looked up from the exclamation point she'd drawn next to the question mark. "Stage? I don't follow."

"The stages of life you've mapped out. Which one are you in at present?"

"Oh." She smiled. "I sort of bypassed the 'we' stage and am bumping around in the 'seed' stage, I think."

"You've never wanted to marry?"

"Sometimes." She wrinkled her nose. "But not to the men who have asked me."

He chuckled at that. "So you want children now?"

"Well, not *right* now, but someday. I'm certainly feeling those urges more often lately. And I adore Mandy."

"You get to spend much time with her?"

"Yes, quite a bit," she admitted, feeling absurdly guilty for enjoying his daughter's company while he'd been deprived of it.

Deprived. What a turnabout! She'd tracked him down to determine why he'd chosen to ignore his daughter and to shame him unmercifully if he still refused to accept Mandy into his life. Two days later, she was guilt ridden and suspicious of her sister.

Regarding his brooding expression as he stared into the fire, Jane found herself wondering about the life he'd carved in these mountains. She'd pictured him as a loner, licking his wounds and feeling sorry for himself. But that scenario was all wrong, she realized. He had come here to find his true self, to recover his values and to live in peace.

"Nic," she said, a thought striking her, "what do you do for money? Are you living off investments?"

"Mostly, but I also have my work."

"What work?"

He looked at her a bit startled. "I'm still an investment counselor."

"You are?"

"Don't look so shocked. The people who really know me trust me and my judgment. After all the publicity died down and Barrett admitted he was a liar, most of my clients went right back to doing business with me."

"But it was rocky there for a while, wasn't it?"

His wide mouth tensed. "It was pure hell, but what doesn't kill you makes you strong. You're looking at Hercules now, sweetheart."

She laughed softly, enjoying his smile.

"I also write a syndicated column called the 'Green Scene' that has been picked up by a few dozen newspapers. It won't start running in them until January."

"I'll watch for it." She tipped her head sideways, eyeing him, speculatively. "You mentioned Barrett Prescott. Is he still in prison?"

"No. He only served six months and paid several million in fines. I don't know what he's up to these days and I don't care. If I see him again in this lifetime, it will be too soon."

She formed a low whistle. "He really burned you, didn't he?"

"He damn near ruined my faith in humanity." He sat up as if suddenly full of nervous energy. "I don't want to dredge that business up again." Bending his knees, he looped his arms around them, mirroring her own posture. His shirt stretched snugly across his wide back and shoulders. "Tell me about Mandy. How does she think I died? By her mother's hands?"

Jane ducked her head to hide her grin. "No. I don't think we've ever really discussed it with her. She just thinks her daddy is in heaven and that's why she never sees him."

"How charming." His tone was murderous.

"Well, we didn't want to tell her that you didn't care about her. Saying you were dead seemed to be the kindest excuse we could come up with."

"Never thought to tell her the truth, huh? That her father didn't know she existed because nobody bothered to inform him."

"And you really didn't know Selena was pregnant? She was showing when you two were going through the dividing up of property in divorce court."

"My attorney handled all that. I never appeared in court."

"Too busy, I guess."

"Selena said she didn't want to see me again and I complied."

Jane leaned back on stiff arms and wrestled again with what she had always thought to be true. Selena had said nothing about telling Nicolas to stay away. Jane was beginning to wonder if he or her sister had ever listened to what the other was saying.

"How can two people love each other and then turn on each other so viciously?" she asked. "I don't mind telling you that your divorce certainly added to my wariness of 'until death us do part' mergers."

"I wasn't aware of your keen interest in my marriage to and divorce from your sister. You were never around."

"Right, but I called home weekly and heard all about the marriage and the breakup."

"One version of it, anyway," he added.

"Yes, I admit it was one-sided."

"And you had a schoolgirl crush on me." He grinned, teasing, his eyes flirting with her.

"Yes, and that's odd."

"Gee, thanks."

"No, I mean, Selena and I never like the same men. Never."

"Well, that record remains intact, in a manner of speaking. I doubt if she likes me."

She gave a nod of concession, then tipped back her head to admire the starry firmament. "The sky looks bigger, brighter, here."

"No pollution or artificial light," he explained.

A howl rent the night and Jane jumped and inched closer to Nic.

"What's that?"

"A timber wolf."

"Really?"

He grinned. "More likely it's a coyote." Yipping barks trailed in from the north. Nic nodded. "Coyote. They sound more like dogs." He leaned his shoulder against hers. "Jane, will you help me to meet Amanda?"

His request filled her with indecision. She closed her eyes, wondering how to squirm out of answering him. She wanted the best for Mandy, but she couldn't keep sneaking around behind Selena's back.

"Things are complicated, Nic," she said haltingly. "I don't know what Selena's thinking right now. After your fax, she's probably figured out that I've opened my big mouth. I asked her where you were living and I'm sure she's recalled that and labeled me a traitor."

"You know Mandy needs me."

He nudged her, giving her a gentle push with his shoulder. She turned her head and met his gaze. Shadows caressed his high cheekbones, his chiseled nose, his strong jawline that was darkened by stubble. His features were classic and stamped with an appealing maturity that hadn't been as evident in the photos she'd seen of him years ago. She admired his muscled forearms and the shape of his hands. Trembling with a fine heat, she looked at his face again. He narrowed his eyes and moistened his lips. She knew the signs and she wanted the kiss he was on the verge of giving her.

"Jane..." He slipped an arm around her back. He bent his head and ran the pad of his thumb across her parted lips. "You're a bewitching creature. You know that?"

"Nic, we shouldn't."

"But you want to."

"Yes, but Mandy..."

"What we're feeling right now has nothing to do with Mandy. I don't know about you, but I'm tired of fighting it. Ever since I tackled you in the woods, I've been telling myself I can't get involved with you."

"You shouldn't. I shouldn't." Her heart was beating like a drum—a primitive rhythm that seemed perfect for this place, this man, this moment.

"Why the hell not?" He stared into her eyes, his thumb stroking her lips. "We're both adults and know what we want, what we crave."

She shook her head. She didn't know. She couldn't think. The rubbing of his thumb upon her lips was driving her wild, and his words...such beautiful words. She clung to his shoulders and pulled him down to her.

The mastery of his kiss alone was enough to give her amnesia. His teeth scraped against her soft, lower lip, then his tongue raced across the satiny skin before dipping inside to tempt and taste. His hands skimmed over her ribs and massaged her supple spine as he drew her more completely into his embrace.

The gentle suckling of his mouth on hers seemed to tug deep within her. She felt her breasts peak as her heartbeats drummed in her ears. Sweet sensations shimmered through her as his beard stubble lightly grazed her cheek. His mouth moved from hers to slide sensuously down the column of her throat. The tip of his tongue blandished and scattered shivers over her skin. Every time he kissed her, she wondered how she'd find the strength to pull away from him, but this time she wondered why she even should. Oh, he was easy to love, to want, to need.

His mouth flamed over hers again and his tongue imitated the act that his body wanted to do with hers. Urgency reigned supreme within her. She felt as if he'd created a whirlpool inside her and that all her good intentions, her morals, her cast-iron rules, were being sucked down and swallowed whole, leaving her pliant and eager.

At last his hand slipped over one of her breasts and his thumb fanned her hard nipple. She writhed and lifted herself toward his touch. He unbuttoned her blouse and his warm hand moved inside, his fingers finding the throbbing nub through the lace and satin of her bra. Somehow, he'd pulled her into his lap, so that she now straddled him. He braced his back against a tree stump. Jane could feel his tumescence against her rump and she moved restlessly upon it.

He tore his mouth from hers. "You're killing me, sweetheart," he growled between gritted teeth. "Don't stop until I'm dead."

His hungry mouth took hers again, stealing her breath and making her want more and more of him. She helped him unbutton her shirt completely and unfasten the front closure of her bra. When her breasts were free, he clamped his lips around one aching nipple while his fingers gently tweaked the other.

Jane clutched at his hair, driving her long fingernails against his scalp and holding his head in place while his magical mouth suckled her, turning her spine to jelly. Her head lolled back and she closed her eyes.

His hips moved beneath her, thrusting, lusting. He slipped a hand over her flat stomach and then between her legs where her yearning had centered, hot and moist. He traced lazy circles there. She released a spate of inarticulate sounds as she lifted up to give him more freedom to rub her, press his hand intimately against her, curve upon her.

This is dangerous, she thought. *Just a little more. One more pass of his hand upon me, one more surge of his tongue against my breast and then I'll stop him.*

The temptation was strong—so strong, one of her hands moved toward his fly before she could snap to attention and rear backward away from him.

"No, Nic. I can't do this. I didn't come here to get...well, you know. I never do this sort of thing and I—it's against my principles." Oh, so sanctimonious! she jeered inwardly as she scrambled to her feet and turned sideways into the shadows to fasten her bra and button her shirt.

She glanced at him and was disconcerted to find him smiling up at her.

"You're pretty when you're all hot and bothered. But I bet you're beautiful after you've been made love to by a man who knows how."

The audacity of that statement sent the blood rushing to her neck and face. "Nic, please."

"What?" His eyes rounded with innocence. "It's the truth."

"The truth is that we've known each other two days and, under the circumstances, we can't get carried away like this. I'm going back to Texas tomorrow to face a very angry woman, who happens to be my sister, and explain to her what I was doing here. I don't want to make that any more difficult than it is already."

"Don't leave tomorrow." He sprang to his feet, graceful as a big cat. "Stay one more day. I have more questions."

"Ask them now."

"I'll take you fishing tomorrow," he said as if he were offering her a diamond necklace.

"Fishing? That's supposed to make me stay?"

"Okay, so we'll laze away the day in the sun. I'll fish, we'll talk, have a picnic lunch and get to know each other better. You can answer all my questions and I'll grill something delicious for dinner. You can postpone your meeting with Hurricane Selena one more day. How's that sound?"

The plan didn't tempt her as much as his smile. "Okay, I guess." Her weak resistance shamed her.

"You guess," he scoffed, drawing a finger along the curve of her cheek. "Why are you fighting this thing between us?"

"I told you. It adds more complications."

"Doesn't have to."

"Yes, it does." She retreated a step. Just the smell of him, a mixture of pine and leather and musky male, made her senses riot.

He curved a hand at the back of her neck, underneath the heavy fall of her hair. "How come a jewelry designer doesn't wear jewelry?"

She blinked, stunned by his quick change of subject. "I do wear it...when I go out. I didn't think it would be appropriate here in the wilds." Jane scrutinized him, reading the question behind his question. "You think I've lied to you? Do you still believe I've come here to do a story on you? Believe me, Thunderheart, if I were a journalist out for a story that would make my career, you wouldn't be on my short list of subjects."

"You think you're pretty tough, don't you?" He pulled her closer, although she stiffened.

"It's late and I'm cold. Let's go inside."

"You're cold?" He spread a hand along her side, his thumb riding under her left breast. "Sweetheart, you're a little furnace, and I'm burning up." He kissed her again, his mouth plucking at hers.

Lethargy invaded her, but she found enough strength to dance out of his range.

"I'm going inside."

"Okay." He shrugged in defeat. "Hey, before you run off, tell me that you'll stay one more day."

"If you have questions, you should have asked me tonight. I have to get back to Dallas. Selena is in a stir, I'm sure, and she—"

"Let her stew for another day. She kept me in the dark for six years, so what's another dark day for her? Big deal." He made a dismissive gesture. "I want to know more about you. What kind of jewelry do you design? Where do you live? And I want to know about Amanda. What's her favorite color? When is her birthday?"

"January sixth. You don't need to know about me, and as for Mandy, I'll answer the other questions over breakfast. Then I'm leaving." She turned and started for the house.

"What happened with your relationship with your father, and why did you decide to come here and tell me about my daughter? Why *now* after six years of silence?" he persisted, never giving up the chase.

With her hand on the doorknob, she paused, trapped. Did he know he'd just asked the twenty-four-thousand-dollar question?

"Jane?" he said softly behind her.

Damn him. "I'll stay one more day," she said wearily. "And then I'm out of here."

"Whatever you say," he rejoined, a smile in his voice.

She jerked open the door and raced upstairs. As she crossed the glassed-in living room, she saw him moving around outside. He doused the camp fire by shoveling dirt and sand on it. He scattered the ashes and firewood, then looked up to catch her watching him.

His teeth flashed in the night as he smiled up at her. Feeling defeated by her own attraction to him, Jane went to the guest bedroom.

She had to think, she told herself as she fell onto the bed with a tortured moan. He had asked some tricky questions and she had to decide how much she was going to tell him. Should she come clean, or hold back vital information? Should she trust him?

Trust him? It was a little beyond that. If she wasn't careful, she'd fall in love with him!

Chapter Seven

Moving through the quiet forest, Nicolas paid heed to the woman following him, understanding that she wasn't used to narrow trails and thick undergrowth.

He could hear her behind him, her steps light, her breathing becoming labored. They'd hiked for almost an hour, checking on his traps. Jane had spent the morning snapping pictures of him and his house to take home with her. They'd talked about Amanda and she'd been quite open with him, answering every question in detail. She'd wanted to go with him on this hike across his land, but he wondered if she was regretting that decision now.

"How are you doing back there?" he asked. "Need to stop a minute?"

"I hate to hold you up..."

Nic shrugged and stopped near an outcropping of rocks. "I'm not on any schedule. Let's rest awhile. I'll even share a granola bar with you."

"Thanks." She wiggled her shapely rump onto a flat rock and sighed. "Ah, that feels nice." Her gaze drifted to his belt where three rabbits dangled. "Do you usually catch all you can eat, or are pickings slim most of the time?''

"Game is plentiful here. I didn't even set the traps again. I probably won't for a few days. Fishing is good right now. When the trout are biting, I don't worry about snaring rabbits or squirrels.''

"I guess you don't need much money to get by out here.''

He nodded. "It's spoiled me. Money is something I don't think about much anymore. Which is ironic, since it used to be my sole reason for getting up in the morning.''

"Life has certainly changed for you.''

He withdrew a granola bar from his knapsack. Unwrapping it and breaking it in half, he handed her one piece and took a bite of the other. "I was glad to have this place when my world crumbled under my feet. This was my oasis, my Eden. I admit, it took some getting used to at first. I was an urban animal and didn't know how to survive for long periods of time without telephones, cars, electricity and constant human companionship.''

"But you adapted,'' Jane observed. "You ever get lonely out here?''

He glanced at her, intrigued by the path of her thoughts. "Sure. Sometimes.''

"I thought you were a hermit, but everybody in town seems to know you there.''

"Not everybody,'' he amended. "I serve on the state wildlife-conservation board, so I've met a few folks that way.'' He didn't like the image she had of him. Selena had certainly fed her a truckload of manure. "I like being alone, but I'm not a loner. The one thing I had the most trouble with at first was getting used to being single again. Even though Selena and I were quits and I knew it was for the best, it was an adjustment. Going from 'we' to 'me' again made me feel even more like a failure. My brother came to visit for the summer five or six months after the divorce was final and I was never so glad to see anyone in my whole life!'' He chuckled, recalling how taken aback Rich had been when greeted at the airport by Nic's big grin and even bigger bear hug.

Jane finished her half of the granola bar and brushed her hands on her jeans. ''Do you still feel the same way about having children?''

''That's a loaded question.'' He leaned back on his arms and looked up through the canopy of tree branches. Sunlight speared his eyes, warmed his face. ''I'm not married or in a relationship so, no, I don't want children. If, however, you're talking about the child I already have . . .'' His gaze collided with hers. ''I want to be part of her life. I want to love her and to be loved by her.''

Jane looked away as if his untarnished admission made her uncomfortable or, perhaps, those were sentimental tears glimmering in her eyes.

''Do you think you'd be a good father to her?''

''Yes, but that's beside the point.''

''How can you say that? Being a good father is the most important—''

''No,'' he interrupted, ''what's important is that I have a right to see my daughter, whether or not you or Selena or anyone else thinks I'm the best father in the world. I'm sure Selena's a good mother, but she didn't have to prove it before she got to see Amanda, did she?''

Jane picked at a bit of moss on the rock. "I see your point. But I feel caught in the middle.''

"Why?"

"I went behind her back. This should have been her decision to see you, not mine.''

"What's done is done. Personally, I think you did the right thing and I'll always be grateful to you for doing it.''

She squared her shoulders and swung one hot-pink tennis shoe. "So, since Selena, has there been anyone special in your life?''

He blinked, startled by her change of subject. "Not really." Grinning, he decided two could play this game. "What about you? Any serious relationships lately?''

"No, not since college.''

"That long ago?"

"It wasn't *that* long ago," she argued, then gave a quick shrug. "But I am due.''

"Overdue, if you ask me.''

She wrinkled her nose in a sassy way. "Nobody asked you. Besides, you can't be too careful nowadays, what with all the nasty germs floating around.''

"Sad, but true." He could appreciate her selectivity. Casual sex had never been interesting or satisfying for him. Sex with Jane, however, interested him immensely. Would she believe him if he told her that in the short time she'd been with him his desire for her had grown tenfold? Probably not. It was difficult even for him to believe.

"What about Selena?" he asked, not really caring about his ex-wife's love life, but needing to get his mind off of bedding Jane. "Who is she seeing these days? Frankly, I'm surprised she hasn't remarried. She's the kind of woman who is happiest when she has a man in the picture."

"Uh, well, she isn't actually *seeing* anyone."

"Oh, yeah? That doesn't sound like her. Is she married to her career?" He laughed at the irony. "That would be fitting. She accused me of that—of course, she was right, but that's beside the point. She hated that I spent so much time with my work and neglected her and our marriage."

"She's very involved with her career," Jane said haltingly. "And she's booked pretty solidly for the next two years with opera productions in the States as well as overseas. She's all the rage in Italy and Japan." She cleared her throat. "You, uh, you haven't kept up with her, have you?"

"I don't scour the newspapers and magazines for her name, no."

"Then you haven't heard."

"Heard what?" He tensed, his mind leaping ahead and seizing on her answer before she spoke it.

"She's married, Nic. Six months ago she married a man who's been part of her life for the past couple of years."

He wasn't bothered by the news of Selena's wedding. What *did* bother him was that Jane had waited so long to tell him. He suspected that Selena's remarriage had something to do with Jane's decision to track him down and see for herself what kind of man had fathered Amanda.

"She's married to Jerome D'Mato. He's a conductor and a composer. Have you heard of him?"

"No, but I'm not a big opera buff."

"Well, he's older than Selena. Twenty-six years older."

He studied her, trying to read her mind through her facial expressions. "You don't approve of that?"

"The age difference is fine by me. Selena needs maturity in her life. And she likes a man who dotes on her and treats her in a fatherly way. Selena's father was very affectionate. Did you know him?"

"Yes, he visited us a few times. Antonio Carr. A big teddy bear of a man, who spoiled her rotten."

"That's him. He died four years ago."

"Yes, I heard about that."

"Selena really missed him until she met Jerome. Antonio used to call Selena 'his little princess' and Jerome calls her 'his queen.'"

"So she's attained the throne," Nic wisecracked. "You've got her pegged. She wants a man who doesn't just love her, but who worships her."

"You didn't?"

"Not enough, obviously." He heard the faint call of an eagle and looked up, trying to find it among the green leaves and the patch of visible sky. "Sometimes it feels as if some other guy married Selena—not me. I know that sounds weird, but that's how I feel. I was a whole other person back then and what I thought I wanted is so different from what I want now."

"Doesn't sound weird to me. People change. Besides, you and Selena married in a whirlwind. You couldn't have known each other well." She gathered her hair into a ponytail and secured it with an elastic band she fished from her shirt pocket. "Jerome was married before, but he's been divorced for a long time. He has grown children and a few grandchildren."

"How is he with Amanda?"

"He's nice to her."

Her choice of words troubled him. "Come on, Jane, I'm already on one hunting expedition, don't send me on another."

Her sigh drifted to him like a leaf on the wind. She eased off the flat rock and sat on the ground across from him, leaning back against the stone. "Jerome is great for Selena, but I'm not so sure he's going to be good for Mandy. I'm worried about her future."

Nic looped his arms around his bent knees, not liking the answers he was getting. "How so? This guy isn't mean to her, is he?"

"No, nothing like that. He's . . . he's indifferent. He doesn't love her, Nic, and I don't think he ever will."

Her expressive eyes shone with truth, and he liked that she was honest with him. Somewhere between last night and this morning, she must have decided to be completely truthful with him.

"He likes Mandy, but that's it. He's crazy for Selena. She's his world. And Selena's new life with Jerome doesn't leave as much time as she used to have for Mandy. He's managing Selena's career and he's booked her solid—even through the holidays."

Nic looked around as he weighed what she'd told him. In the distance he heard a flutter of wings and a sharp cry of startled birds. He scowled, wondering what creature had upset the covey.

Turning his attention back to Jane, he found that she'd removed one shoe and was adjusting her pink sock.

"How does Selena feel about all of this?" he asked.

"She's thrilled. She loves to work and be in demand." Jane put her tennis shoe back on. "She's wanted this for a long time, and she's very much in love with Jerome. They both are passionate about the opera and music. They love to travel and would rather live in hotels than in a house. The cocktail parties, the premieres, the rehearsals, the benefits—they thrive on all that stuff." She made a cast-off gesture with one hand. "But where does that leave Mandy?"

"Right. Where *does* my daughter fit in?"

Jane chewed thoughtfully on her lower lip. "I don't know, and that's what worries me."

"That's why you picked this time to come find me."

"Yes." Her eyes met his briefly. "I decided to find you for Mandy's sake." She laced up her shoe slowly, and Nic sensed she avoided his gaze on purpose. After a moment, she cleared her throat. Her body language told him she was uneasy in her thoughts. "My father never had anything to do with me and that hurt, especially when Selena's dad visited and showered her with gifts and affection. I always wanted a father's love, and I want Mandy to have that, too. I hoped Selena would eventually remarry and give Mandy a father, but Jerome has raised his children and isn't interested in raising another child.'' Her gaze finally bounced up to his and she smiled shyly. ''He's in the 'me' stage again, you see. He's past his 'seed' stage—way past it.''

''Isn't Selena worried about this?''

''She's downplaying it, but I think she's concerned. Last month Jerome made some calls to boarding schools, and Selena was upset about that.''

Nic gritted his teeth. ''Boarding schools?'' He didn't like the sound of that. It smacked of a mother choosing her new husband over her own child.

''Selena was dead set against that—''

''Thank God,'' Nic interjected.

''But now she's talking about how one of the schools is nice and how Mandy will like it. I hate to see Mandy carted off to boarding school at such a young age. I've offered to keep her some, and Mother baby-sits, but Selena and Jerome are gone for months at a time now and Mandy can't miss that much school.''

''Do you believe Selena will actually place her in a boarding school?''

She hesitated before answering. ''I didn't think so,'' she said slowly, ponderously, ''but last week she told me she was going to check on one school in Maryland again. She said Jerome was pressing her to enroll Mandy after Christmas vacation.''

Nic stood, his muscles twitching with his burst of irritation. ''Oh, that's just great.'' A dull anger pounded behind his eyes. ''She's only a baby, for crying out loud. How can Selena send her off to Maryland? Jane, you've got to talk to her and make her see it's only fair that I spend time with my daughter. Why send Mandy to Maryland, when she can live here with me?''

"Are the schools good in Asheville?"

"The best, and the elementary school principal is a friend of mine."

"She'd love it out here. She's like me that way. She appreciates the outdoors. She's a nature girl. I take her hiking and biking. She's a ball of energy."

"Then you'll talk to Selena." He held out his hands. She stared at him a moment before placing her hands in his and letting him pull her to her feet.

"It won't be easy discussing you with her, Nicolas. I'm sure she's furious with me for dredging all this up."

"I don't care about that. Her temper tantrums are legendary, but once she has screamed her lungs out, she fizzles."

Jane nodded, conceded his logic. "I might be able to convince her that you've changed and that you both should let bygones be bygones. Maybe you two can agree on joint custody."

"I have no problem with that. One way or another, I'm going to see my daughter."

She placed her hands on his arms. "Nic, please let me handle this. Don't stir up the waters or you'll ruin everything."

He started to tell her that he wasn't concerned with making waves, but another squawk yanked his attention from her. He peered through the green-and-gold foliage, then glanced up to see the tip of an outstretched wing. An eagle. Leaves rustled as small animals scurried. The hair at the back of his neck stood on end. He stepped away from Jane as his instincts came into play.

"Stay here." Nic moved away from her, careful not to make too much noise.

"Where are you—"

He waved her into silence and sent her a dark scowl that smothered the rest of her questions, then he stalked forward, his ears and eyes tuned to the whispers of the forest.

They'd tracked close to the turnoff to the highway. Nic smelled exhaust fumes and could hear the whisking sound of traffic. Crouching as he ran, he brushed aside branches, his feet falling silently, his breathing regulated. He slowed, sensing someone ahead of him, and peered through the underbrush. A man was getting into a black pickup. Nic moved closer to read the North Carolina license plate. He filed it to memory.

Scouting the area, he found a few feathers, but no spent shell casings or signs of a kill. Satisfied, he retraced his steps to Jane. Sitting on the rock again, her chin cradled in one hand, she greeted him with a belligerent frown.

"What was that all about? Answering the call of the wild?"

Nic grinned. "I heard someone."

"I don't like it when you run off like that, Thunderheart. Remember that I don't know where I am, how to get anywhere or which way is up out here. It's scary when you tell me to stay—"

"I think it was the hunter who has been trespassing and trying to bag an eagle."

Her eyes rounded. "Did you see him?" She slipped off the rock, the frown gone.

He nodded and tapped his forehead. "I've got his license plate number right up here. I'll radio the game warden when we get back home."

"But you have no proof he was shooting at eagles, so what good will that do?"

"I have proof he was trespassing," Nic explained. "The game warden will keep an eye out for the guy and follow him. With any luck, he'll catch him in the act. If not, he'll arrest him for trespassing."

"It's just one exciting thing after another out here, isn't it?"

Nic chuckled and draped an arm around her shoulders. "Whatever you say, Lady Jane."

The endearment slipped out as natural as his own breath. He felt her sharp glance, but then she smiled and eased an arm around his waist. They walked side by side until the path grew too narrow, then Nic took her by the hand and led the way through heaps of fallen leaves and tangles of brush. When the house came into view, he heard her give a soft whoop of relief. Glancing back, he grinned at her flushed face and pulled her to stand beside him.

"I propose that I rustle up some supper while you— rest your hot-pink toesies."

She laughed and gave his waist a squeeze. "You sweet talker, you. I accept your proposal, Thunderheart. The kitchen's all yours."

Thunderheart. He knew what she was doing. He'd called her Lady Jane and she was responding with his last name. The unspoken message was: nothing personal.

Not Nicolas anymore, or even Nic. Thunderheart. One of the guys. He gave a short sigh. Silly game, he thought, and it wouldn't change how he felt about her, or how she felt about him.

LYING AWAKE THAT NIGHT in the guest bedroom, Jane wondered for the hundredth time if she was doing the right thing by telling Nic about the boarding school.

Maybe she was being selfish and sticking her nose where it didn't belong. She adored her niece, but Selena was Mandy's mother and it was her business where Mandy went to school. However, Jane knew Selena well, and she could tell that Selena wasn't convinced about sending Mandy away. Jerome was putting pressure on her, and she wanted this marriage to work and to last. But should Mandy's happiness be sacrificed just because Jerome didn't want to be a parent?

Flinging off the covers, she left the bed and paced to the window where moonlight bled through the tree branches.

Dinner had been delicious, and she'd enjoyed it after soaking her feet in the stream. The fried rabbit, baked acorn squash and hush puppies had been the best she'd ever tasted. Nicolas had regaled her with tales of his trials and tribulations while building his house. In turn, she had told him about a camping trip she'd taken with Mandy last year and the rainstorm that had collapsed their tent in the middle of the night.

She felt closer to him than ever, but the cloud of her imminent departure hung over her. The intensity of her feelings for him was both alarming and thrilling. She knew that he was struggling with the same emotions and that added to her excitement.

Back in college she'd been infatuated with Nicolas and proud to claim him as part of the family. But being with him now had nothing to do with what she'd felt for him then. These sensations were those of a woman who knew her own heart, her own mind. She was a woman who recognized a man who could pleasure her and satisfy her. Making love with Nicolas would be . . . But she couldn't. She shouldn't. Complicating an already dangerous relationship wouldn't help anyone.

The beauty of the night tempted her and she slipped into her silky white robe and stuck her feet into the matching mules. Padding downstairs, she escaped outside and went around the house to the patio. The night air was cool, almost too chilly, and she thought about going back inside for a blanket.

A sudden movement near one of the patio chairs made her heart stutter, and for a panicked moment she thought the bear had returned for more honey rolls.

"You look like a shapely night ghost in that robe," Nicolas said, rising from one of the roomy chairs he'd hewn from massive logs.

Jane placed a hand over her pounding heart. "You gave me a start! What are you doing out here?"

"Looking at the stars and thinking. Guess you couldn't sleep, either."

"I'm restless," she confessed. Jeans hugged his hips and legs, but he was barefoot and shirtless. "Aren't you chilly?"

"Nope." He sat in the chair again and linked his hands behind his head. His chest was lightly furred and heavily muscled. His underarms were smooth, nearly hairless. "Feels good to me."

Looks good to me, Jane thought with a secret smirk. She tightened the belt of her robe and glanced around at the silvery night. A breeze whispered through the pines and ruffled the hem of her gown and robe. She eyed the chair past Nic's and made her way to it, but as she drew even with him, he snagged her hand and pulled her into his lap.

"Hey! What do you think you're doing?" she asked, laughing. His body felt wonderfully warm against hers, much better than any blanket could have felt. "Let me up."

"Uh-uh." He shook his head and tightened his arms around her. "Are you sure you want to leave tomorrow?"

"Yes. I planned to be away a day or two, tops. I have a life and a job back in Dallas, you know."

"Yes, but do you really want to leave?"

"Nic, don't do this." She pressed her hands against his shoulders. "I have to leave, and that's that."

"Will you come back?"

She stared at the flames of hope dancing in his eyes and her heart thudded sweetly. Should she trust this feeling? she wondered desperately. "Do you want me to?"

"Sure, and I want you to bring Amanda with you."

The eddying thrill diminished within her and she felt foolish. Could he be using her to get to his daughter?

She hated the question and the sliver of mistrust that came with it. She so wanted to trust this man.

"You *are* going to talk to Selena, aren't you?"

"Yes, now let me up." She squirmed, but he held her in his lap.

"Not so fast, Lady Jane." His lips touched her neck as his hands splayed warmly at her back and hip. "This is our last night together for a while. Let's make the most of it."

"No, Nic."

"You know why we're both restless, don't you?" He nuzzled the underside of her jaw. "When I close my eyes, all I can see is you. It's been so long since I've felt like this about anyone." He blew in her ear and his tongue tickled behind it.

How did he know the location of every one of her hot spots? she wondered disjointedly as his lips found another along the curve of her shoulder. His fingers fastened on the knotted belt of her robe and loosened it. She tried to form a sufficient protest, but he chose that moment to cover her mouth with his and the words melted like butter under a flame. She'd never known a man so attuned to her body. His big hands gentled her, fevered her, explored her. She was no longer cold, but burning hot as his mouth fed off hers. She moaned fretfully when his tongue breached her lips and mated with hers.

His nimble fingers moved around her breasts, across them, his palms whispering over the fabric of her gown. Her nipples poked into his palms. He squeezed her breasts and she arched into him. She grew moist and achy. Before she was hopelessly lost to him, Jane pulled away and managed to scramble from his lap. Standing before him, she tightened her belt and her reserve.

"What is it, Jane? Is it Selena? Do you think she'd object to this?"

"Oh, I *know* she would," Jane said with a laugh. "But not because of what you're thinking. She would object because she'd see this as me taking your side. I don't want to make love to you, Nic, because it will only cloud the issue of Mandy and what's best for her. I want to keep a clear head and a clear heart about this."

"I want what's best for Mandy, too, but I can't deny that I want you, Jane." He stared at her and seemed to note the seriousness in her because he visibly backed off, leaning away from her and crossing his hands behind his head. "Okay. When you're right, you're right. Damn it."

She smiled at his halfhearted curse. "It's too fast, Nic. We need some time apart. We need time to think."

He stared up at the heavens, nodding slowly. She could tell he was convincing himself that she was right again. Logic was winning out over his need to mate. He grimaced good-naturedly and emitted a playful growl of exasperation.

"Okay, okay." He held up his hands in surrender. "You're worth waiting for, Lady Jane."

She smiled and some of the tension left her body. "I'm glad you think so."

He smiled at her, a smile that lit up his face and made her heart lodge in her throat. "Would you like for me to walk you back to your bedroom?"

"No." She retreated as if he were temptation itself. "You stay put."

"Okay," he said, giving her a slow wink. "I sure like that outfit. You look like a walking dream."

Jane focused her attention on his mouth and memories of his kisses whirled through her.

"Sweet dreams, Lady Jane," he whispered, his voice a purr.

She went back to her room, each step away from him an effort. Tomorrow would come too soon she knew and she dreaded it. She'd found something special in this remote region and his name was Nicolas Thunderheart.

Chapter Eight

"Benedict Arnold!"

"Selena, please hear me out." Jane held out her hands in desperation, thinking that her sister looked like a spitting cat. "I know you're mad at me, but I was thinking of Mandy."

"Mad at you? Ha! I *loathe* you," Selena said in her most dramatic tone and the trace of a British accent that she had "acquired" when she was fourteen without having ever stepped foot in England. "And how dare you say that you were thinking of Mandy. My daughter does not need your interference."

Jane dropped into one of the roomy chairs in Selena's all-white living room. Through a plate-glass window, she could see Jerome diving off the springboard and into a lagoon-shaped swimming pool. "I only wanted to check Nicolas out, to see if he'd changed. If he wants to be a part of his daughter's life, then how can you keep him from her?"

"How? You just watch me, little sister, and you'll see how." Selena tossed her head, making her long light brown hair shimmer over her shoulders. "He won't be allowed near her."

"Why not?"

"Because he never wanted her, that's why."

"That's a lie, Selena."

"Wh-what?" She narrowed her hazel eyes. "How dare you! He's already turned you against me, I see. I'm disappointed in you, Jane. I thought you'd be more loyal."

"It's not a matter of loyalty. You told us that—"

"Hellooo!" Estelle Frazier's cheerful voice interrupted them. "We're back."

"Mommy, Grammy bought me a *Beauty and the Beast* lunch box," Mandy announced as she raced into the living room ahead of her grandmother. She released a little squeal of joy when she saw Jane. "Aunt Jane's here! Goody! Goody!"

"Come here, scamp, and give me a hug." Jane opened her arms and embraced her niece. She smiled as her mother entered the room. "Hi, Mom. You've changed your hair."

Estelle patted her shorter gray locks. "Oh, yes. I had it cut. What do you think?"

"I love it. Don't you like it, Selena?"

Selena arched a brow. "Don't change the subject, Jane."

"What's the subject?" Estelle asked, glancing from daughter to daughter. "Oh, *that* subject. There's nothing like a good cat fight over a man. I hope I haven't missed the first round."

"There isn't going to be a fight," Jane said. She ran a hand over Mandy's dark brown hair and thought of Nicolas. A sad yearning settled in her heart. She'd been away from him for two days, but it seemed much longer. "Let me see your new lunch pail, Mandy."

Mandy pulled the plastic box out of a bag. Her green eyes sparkled. "Isn't it neat?"

"Mother, why are you buying her a lunch box?" Selena asked in a bored tone. "Adamsley School feeds its students."

"You haven't given in to Jerome on this, have you?" Estelle sat on the long, white brocade couch. "Have you asked Mandy what she wants?"

"I'm not going anywhere," Mandy said, worry pinching the skin between her eyes. "Am I, Mommy?"

Selena gave a shake of her head. "Mandy, honey, take your things upstairs and call Becky. She wants to invite you to her birthday party this Saturday."

"All riiight!" Mandy kissed her grandmother. "I love my lunch box. I'm taking it to school Monday. Christine will pack me a lunch, won't she, Mommy?"

"Of course. Just tell her in plenty of time. You know how she is. She doesn't like surprises." Selena selected a mint from a crystal candy dish adorning the top of the white baby grand piano. "Domestics are so independent these days."

Jane looked at her mother and smiled. She knew that Estelle was also thinking that it hadn't been all that long ago since Selena had no idea about domestics or chefs or any other such household help.

"Stay here," Mandy ordered, giving Jane a kiss. "I'll be right back."

"I'm not budging an inch," Jane promised, giving Mandy a pat on the seat of her plaid shorts.

Amanda skipped out of the room to the wide staircase in the front foyer.

"When did you get back, Jane?" Estelle asked.

"This morning. I came right over to talk to Jane."

"A wise move. She screamed like she'd passed a bowling ball when she got that fax from Nic."

"Mother!" Selena rolled her eyes. "Where do you come up with those crude expressions?"

"I got that one from your husband. It was *his* description. I'm only repeating it."

Selena's teeth clicked together and her face paled. Jane bit her lip to keep from laughing aloud. She shared a humor-laden wink with her mother.

"Can you blame me for screaming when my own sister stabs me in the back?"

"I only wanted to see Nic for myself and to give him a piece of my mind."

"Oh, that's rich," Selena said, sitting on the other end of the long couch. "I thought you were over your fascination for him."

"*I am.*" Hearing her almost strident tone, Jane winced inwardly. "This had nothing to do with that. I decided to confront him since you wouldn't."

"I don't want him meddling in my life. You had no right to talk to him without speaking to me first."

"I have spoken to you about him," Jane reminded her. "Selena, he's not as bad as you said. He didn't even know about Mandy."

"Selena, is this true?" Estelle asked, regarding her critically. "Didn't you tell him about your pregnancy?"

Selena shrugged her tanned shoulders, exposed by her sleeveless sun suit. Summer was making a last stand and it was still blazingly hot in Dallas, making Jane wish for the cooler mountain air of the Smokies.

"Selena . . ." Estelle sharpened her gaze on her eldest daughter. "Have you been lying to us all this time? Whatever for? How could you do this?"

"He didn't want a child," Selena snapped. "I told you that."

"He doesn't deny that," Jane said. "Your marriage was shaky and his business was in jeopardy. But you told us that he knew about the pregnancy and that he turned his back on you. Nic says you never told him. He was shocked and mad as hell when I convinced him that he had a daughter."

"Of course he was mad," Selena insisted. "He never wanted a child."

"But he wants to see her."

Selena's face hardened. "Oh, yes? He's using Mandy as an excuse to see me. I don't want him using my child as a pawn."

Jane shook her head. "I don't think his wanting to see Mandy has anything to do with you."

"You've just met him and you think you know what's going on in his devious mind? He wants to make my life miserable and you've given him a means by which to do it."

"For heaven's sake, Selena," Estelle scolded, "it's been years since your divorce. Do you really think Nic has been holding a torch all this time? And why would he want to make you miserable? He hasn't been making a pest of himself. You haven't heard a peep from him in ages."

"Whose side are you on?" Selena demanded.

"Mandy's."

"Me, too," Jane chimed in. "That's why I went and I'm glad I did. Selena, he has a beautiful place in the Smokies. It's *not* a bridge to nowhere."

"It's in the middle of nowhere," Selena insisted.

"No, it's in the middle of a lovely forested area near a wildlife reserve. The house is big and comfortable. Nic isn't a bitter recluse. He's made lots of friends and he's involved in various things in Asheville, the nearest town. Here, I had some photos developed." Jane pulled the packet from her purse. "Okay, here we go. See..." she handed Selena one of the snapshots... "—this is his house. Isn't it the most gorgeous thing you've ever seen?"

Selena gave a sniff and passed the photo to Estelle. "It's interesting."

"Here are some others. Here's Nicolas and the smokehouse, and this is a picture of the stream. That's some of the bird feeders and birdhouses he built." She handed over the photos, which Selena examined before passing them on to Estelle. "As you can see by the photographs, the inside of the house is as beautiful as the outside. Mom, that's the guest bedroom. Nicolas made the furniture. It's Shaker."

"He has certainly won you over." Selena raked Jane with her sultry gaze. "I don't care if he lives in a castle and has hot and cold running servants—he isn't getting Mandy."

"You'd rather send her away to some stuffy, old boarding school than let her get to know her father?" Jane demanded. "Selena, are you sure you're thinking of Mandy's best interests?"

"I haven't decided about the boarding school. Jerome and I are going to go on a tour of it next week and then we'll see."

"You shouldn't let your husband lead you around by the nose," Estelle said. "You won't be happy in this marriage by being his rubber stamp."

Jane grinned. "Maybe that's why you've been married six times, Mom. You're too independent for marriage."

Estelle grimaced at being reminded of her many trips to the altar. "Perhaps, but what I lacked in the wife department I made up for in the mother department. Selena, your first responsibility is to Amanda. That child won't be happy in a boarding school. She's been around loving family all her life and she'll miss that terribly if she's sent away to live with strangers."

Selena surged up from the couch, all drama and flair as she flounced to the center of the room and tipped up her chin in a gesture of affront. "I won't have you two ganging up on me. I know what's best for my child."

"We're not ganging up on you," Jane said wearily. "I'm trying to tell you that Nicolas has changed."

"Ha! A lot you know."

"From the looks of these photographs, I'd say he has his act together. That place of his is really something." Estelle gave the pictures back to Jane, who returned them to her purse.

"Selena, he's not the person you described to me," Jane said. "He wants to meet Amanda—"

"I don't care what he wants."

"And he doesn't want to have to resort to the court system to do it," Jane finished, and received the reaction she expected. Both her mother and sister stared at her as if she'd announced the end of the world. "It would be better if you hashed this out with Nic and kept the attorneys out of it, Selena. Better for you and for Mandy."

"He's threatening to take me to court."

"Not exactly. He's ready to talk sensibly right now, but if you stonewall him, Selena, he'll come out fighting."

"Do you hear that, Mother?" Selena turned to Estelle and gestured toward Jane. "Now do you think Nic's not out to make me miserable?"

"He's not," Jane insisted. "He's only demanding his rights as a father. Selena, he wants to be part of Mandy's life. Why is that so terrible? If my father had insisted on seeing me, I would have been thrilled. I'm sure Mandy will be anxious to meet him after you tell her—"

"I'm not going to tell her," Selena cut in. "He's dead to Amanda and he's staying that way." Her expressive eyes took on a hard glitter. "He insinuated that I'd make just as lousy a parent as he'd tried to be to his younger brother. Well, I've shown him that he's wrong. Amanda is an angel."

"Selena, this might be just what you need," Estelle said. "If you and Jerome are going to be busy touring the first part of next year, you won't have to put Mandy in a boarding school if Nicolas agrees to take her. With Nic, she'll still be with her family.''

"No." Selena fairly shook with agitation. "If he gets his mitts on her, he'll turn her against me. He'll convince everyone that I'm a horrible mother because I chose my career over my daughter."

"How could he turn Mandy against you?" Jane asked dubiously. "You're giving him way too much credit."

"He's already turned *you* against me."

"No, he hasn't," Jane argued, exasperated.

"Oh, please." Selena rolled her eyes. "Don't you think I know the symptoms, Jane? I've been there, dear. I know how charming and seductive he can be. You thought he was some kind of American hero, and it's obvious to me that you still do."

"You're wrong. I'm not starry-eyed over him. Having her father in her life would be great for Amanda and I think—"

"Shh." Selena hissed, motioning toward the foyer where Amanda's footsteps could be heard. "She's coming in here and I don't want one word said in front of her about him."

Jane nodded reluctantly and Estelle gave a helpless shrug. Round one was over, but the match had just begun, Jane thought. She'd have to convince her sister that she wasn't taking Nic's side in this battle. She was thinking only of her niece's welfare. A twinge of conscience brought her up short. She *was* thinking only of Amanda, she argued, then realized that she shouldn't have to be trying to convince herself. Selena had hit upon a glimmer of truth, Jane admitted grudgingly.

Nic had impressed her, but she wasn't starry-eyed over him.

Yet.

THE RAINBOW-PATTERNED comforter brought a smile of satisfaction to Jane's face. She admired the pastel-colored bedroom she had decorated expressly for her niece, imagining Mandy's delight with the new bed linens, coverlet and sham pillows. Mandy had spent many nights in either Jane's or Estelle's extra bedrooms since Selena had married Jerome D'Mato.

Once again Selena and Jerome were leaving for Los Angeles to iron out some business details. Instead of jerking Mandy out of school, they had decided to let her stay with Jane, even though the time would include the Thanksgiving holiday.

"We've been invited to spend Thanksgiving with friends in Aspen," Selena had explained to Jane. "These people are huge opera benefactors and we just couldn't refuse. Besides, we deserve some time off, and after Thanksgiving we have a very busy period coming up with back-to-back performances in New York and Rome."

Jane had heard the guilt in Selena's voice, knowing that her sister would have hired a tutor and taken Mandy with her if not for Jerome. Her new husband was glad to have his children raised, and while he doted on Selena, he was careful not to get too close to Mandy.

The phone's metallic ring cut through her musings. Probably Selena saying she's running late, Jane thought as she went into the living room and picked up the receiver.

"Hello?" She dropped into an easy chair in the living room and draped one leg over the arm.

"Hello, stranger."

Nic's deep, resonant voice stroked her nerve endings. Jane pressed a hand over her heart, which had kicked into double time.

"Nic? Wh-where are you calling from?"

"Don't panic. I'm in Asheville on a pay phone."

She closed her eyes in relief. Was her tone such a dead giveaway? Obviously, he knew he had her on the ropes.

"How are things going there?" he asked.

"Oh, fine. How are you?"

"I'm not asking about your health, Jane," he drawled. "What's Selena up to? Did you talk any sense into her?"

"Nic, this is going to take some time. Selena's stubborn and she's got it in her head that you're out to harm her. She can't forget that you didn't want to be a parent."

"Well, that's irrelevant, don't you think? I mean, I *am* a parent, so we can move on to the next objection." His sigh of exasperation bled across the phone line. "I can't believe that she's still mired in the past. Sure, I wasn't ready to be a parent back then. After botching it big-time when my brother needed me, I had serious doubts about my parenting abilities—and hers. But that's water under the bridge. I'm older and wiser and I'm definitely in my 'seed' phase to quote a cut-rate philosopher."

Grinning, she snuggled deeper into the chair cushions. Hearing his voice again was a mixed blessing. Her senses craved him and every syllable he spoke pleased her, seduced her. But more than miles separated them.

"You believe me, don't you?"

"Yes." But should she? Was he snowing her? Was he using her to get to his child? If he was, who could blame him?

"You know, I should be mad at you."

"Mad? Why?" she asked.

"You sashayed into my life, turned it upside down and then left me to clean up the mess."

"I had to get back here and clean up a bigger mess."

"Have you?"

"I'm working on it." She wound the curly phone cord around her forefinger.

"I'm growing impatient."

"It's only been a couple of weeks."

"I have a lot of time to catch up on."

"Yes, I know." She shifted uneasily in the chair.

"I thought I'd visit during Thanksgiving."

"No." Jane sat up with a bolt of panic and almost jerked the phone off the occasional table.

"Why not? School's out and—"

"Mandy won't be here," she lied, surprised at how quickly and easily deception sprang to her lips.

"Where will she be?"

"Uh, Selena and Jerome are staying with friends over the holiday."

"This is all so damned unfair." His voice throbbed with overwrought emotion. "Selena's spent all these holidays with our daughter while I've been alone. I didn't want to spend another holiday without meeting her. I thought if I came there and talked to Selena, she might agree to letting me see Amanda without a big fight. Is she going to make me take this to the courts, Jane?"

"No, Nic. I'm begging you to give me a little more time. When they get back from their holiday trip, I'll talk to Selena again. Right now she's upset at me for going behind her back and telling you about Amanda. Let's give her time to cool off."

"Well, what about you?" he asked wearily.

"I forgive you for sending that fax."

"No, that's not what I meant. What are you doing for Thanksgiving? Do you have any plans?"

Oh, no. He was going to ask her to spend Thanksgiving with him, and she wanted to, but she couldn't because she had lied about Mandy's holiday plans. The irony of her situation placed a grim smile on her lips.

"I'm spending Thanksgiving with Mom," she said, which was partly true. Estelle and her current paramour, a retired chef, were hosting a feast for family and friends at a trendy supper club.

"I see. I was hoping you'd join me here for Thanksgiving."

"It's sweet of you to ask." The thought of him spending the holiday alone in his beautiful, peaceful house squeezed her heart and stung her eyes. "I wish . . ." She wouldn't let herself finish the statement, afraid he would ask her again and she'd forget that she would have Mandy with her.

"If you change your mind, I'll be here."

"Thanks. Why don't you ask Abby to join you?"

"She will be visiting her son and daughter in Charleston."

"Oh." She fought off her own weakness. "Maybe that bear will show up for a feast."

He chuckled briefly. "Maybe, but I imagine he's found himself a cave and is fast asleep. Hey, have a good holiday." He'd forced a lighter note to his voice. "I won't keep you any longer."

"Thanks for calling, Nic, and I promise I'll talk to Selena."

"And I'll get back to you after Thanksgiving," he tacked on, his tone firm. "I can't wait indefinitely."

"I know."

"Okay. Well, goodbye, Jane."

"'Bye, Tarzan." She heard his deep chuckle before the line clicked and went dead. Jane replaced the receiver reluctantly, her mind far away in the heart of the Smokies.

The chiming of the doorbell brought her back to her duplex in Dallas and out of the comfortable chair. She opened the door to a smiling Amanda and a harried Selena.

"We're running late, as usual," Selena said, turning to wave to the driver in a white stretch limousine. "He's going to pick up Jerome at the office and then come back here for me."

"Come on in." Jane took one of the suitcases from Selena. A refreshing breeze came inside with her guests. "Feels like autumn is finally making an entrance, and it's about time."

"I packed sweaters for Mandy and her corduroy pants, just in case." Selena went through the house, heading for the spare bedroom.

"Mom, come look at my room. Aunt Jane, I *love* this bedspread," Mandy called to them.

Selena glanced back at Jane. "You didn't buy her more things, did you?"

"Just a comforter, pillows, stuff like that." Jane shrugged. "They were on sale at Neiman Marcus."

Selena dropped the overnight bag and small suitcase just inside the door. "Very pretty," she said, walking to the bed and touching the rainbow comforter with her long red nails. "Remember your manners, Amanda."

"Thank you, thank you, thank you!" Mandy held out her arms, then wrapped them around Jane's neck for a hug and kiss.

Jane laughed. "You're welcome, scamp."

"I want to listen to the old records," Mandy said, heading for the ancient stereo that had been Jane's when she was a kid.

Amanda had developed a passion for Jane's collection of Disney film soundtracks. And she loved the old vinyl LPs or "platters" as she and Jane called them.

"Listen to your heart's content," Jane encouraged her, then went to join Selena in the living room. "I think it might be time to introduce her to Elvis. I bet she'd love his old records."

Selena sent her an arched glance. "Jane, dear, *all* of his records are old."

"You know what I mean—his early recordings." She motioned to the chairs and chintz-covered sofa. "Have a seat."

"She has an ear for music," Selena said, choosing to sit on the sofa. "Jerome says she can take piano at Adamsley."

Jane gritted her teeth. "How can you keep talking about that place as if it's heaven on earth? Selena, you know that Mandy won't like it there."

"I don't know any such thing. I've seen it and it's quite posh."

"You haven't asked her if she wants to go there."

"I'm her mother and I will decide that."

"Jerome has decided it."

Selena sent her a warning glare. "You sound like Mother now. Jerome does not control me."

"Will you think about letting her see Nic?"

"There is nothing to think about."

"Oh, yes, there is. He isn't going away, Selena. Now that he knows, he is bound and determined to see Mandy."

"And I have you to thank for that," Selena said coldly.

"He would have found out about Mandy eventually. He'd read something about her or see her picture—"

"And assumed that I'd adopted a child or had one by some other man besides him."

"Not if he saw her picture," Jane argued. "She looks like him."

Selena drummed her long fingernails on the couch arm. "Yes, you're right," she agreed, tight-lipped. "Okay, Jane, I'll consider this problem while I'm away."

"Sis, if he and Mandy hit it off, then he could help you take care of her while you're on tour."

"Why are you so opposed to the boarding school?"

"Because it will feel to Mandy as if you're getting rid of her—that you've chosen Jerome and dumped her."

"That's nonsense."

"No, it's common sense. How would you have felt if Mom had shipped you off after one of her marriages?"

A horn tooted outside and Selena rose from the couch. "That'll be Jerome in the limo. I've got to run." She angled closer to Jane and lowered her voice to a whisper. "You honestly think he'd be a good father to her?"

"All I know at this point is that he *wants* to be a good father to her, which is more than I can say for Jerome."

Selena gave a long sigh. "I do wish Jerome would—"

"You leaving now, Mommy?" Mandy asked, skipping into the room.

"Yes, dear. Give me a big kiss." Selena gathered Mandy into her arms and hugged her fiercely, then gave her a kiss. "I'll miss you terribly."

"I'll be okay, Mommy."

"I know." Selena smiled at Jane. "I'm leaving you in good hands." She set Mandy on her feet and bussed

Jane on the cheek. "Take care. I'll call you after Thanksgiving."

"Okay, but we'll be in and out." Jane saw her to the door.

"I know. You two will probably go to all those awful Christmas sales during the holiday."

"Movies, too," Mandy added. "There are a bunch of good movies starting."

"Well, have fun." Selena wiggled the fingers of her left hand in a high-society wave. Sunlight flashed in her three-carat wedding ring set.

Jane and Mandy waved as the limo pulled away from the curb. Closing the door, Jane looked down into Mandy's green eyes. She thought of Nic alone on Thanksgiving. Would she dare risk another demonstration of Selena's wrath?

"Aunt Jane, have you been to Adamsley?"

A knot tightened in Jane's throat. "No."

"Why do I have to go there?"·

"You don't, scamp, not if you don't want to." She knew she was playing with fire and making promises she wasn't sure she could keep.

Mandy sighed. "Will you help me unpack?"

Jane squatted in front of Mandy, taking her by the hands and facing her. "How would you like to take a trip? I know of a beautiful place in the mountains where we could spend the holiday. You and me and a friend of mine. He has a lovely house near a stream. There are fish and birds and deer. It will be fun!"

"What about Grammy?"

"Grammy won't mind." *Mommy, on the other hand, will be livid.*

"We could leave after school is out?"

"Yes, that's right. We'll leave Wednesday evening."

Mandy grinned, showing gaps where baby teeth had been. "Your friend won't care if you bring me along?"

"Oh, honey, my friend will be *thrilled* to meet you." She framed Mandy's endearing face in her hands and prayed she was doing the right thing.

Chapter Nine

Abby Masters forged the trail, her sturdy legs carrying her across the uneven ground, her walking stick pushing aside branches and tall grass.

"It was lucky I saw you in town," Jane said, trailing Abby with Amanda in the middle. "I wasn't at all sure I could find my way back to Nic's."

"That's one of the reasons we like this living arrangement," Abby said, pausing to let them catch up. "Hardly any surprise visitors." She placed a hand on top of Amanda's shoulder, then gave the bill of the child's baseball cap a tug. "I'll bet he'll be glad to see you two, though. I'm leaving tomorrow to spend Thanksgiving with my kids and I hated to think of Nic being here all alone through the holiday."

"Do you usually spend holidays with him?" Jane asked.

Abby adjusted her gaily-colored sun visor. "Sometimes, depending on the weather. My kids visit here a lot and Nic's always welcome at my table. But my daughter-in-law had a baby three months ago, so I agreed to do the traveling this time."

"A baby? Boy or girl?" Amanda asked.

"A boy. Travis Ryan. Nine pounds, two ounces at birth. Twenty-one inches."

"Someday I'm going to have a brother or sister," Amanda stated. "Someday soon, I hope."

Jane gave her a skeptical look, certain that Selena had made no such promise to Amanda. She chalked it up to a child's wishful thinking.

"Jane, I think you can find your way from here," Abby said, pointing ahead with her walking stick. "Nic's house is straight through here. See how the foliage has been pushed aside to make a sort of trail? Keep to that. Another half mile and you'll hear the stream up ahead."

Giving a nod, Jane held out her hand. "Thanks again, Abby. Have a wonderful Thanksgiving."

"Same to you." Abby shook her hand, then gave Amanda's head a pat. "Give Nic a hug and a kiss for me!"

Jane watched the older woman head to the east and hoped she was as healthy and independent at Abby's age. Amanda slipped her hand within Jane's.

"She's nice."

"Yes, she's a gem," Jane agreed. "Well, it's just you and me again, kiddo. It's not much farther to Nic's, so let's go." Jane took the lead, walking slowly enough for Mandy to keep up with her.

She hadn't notified Nic of her decision to join him for Thanksgiving. Anxiety coiled tightly in her chest, shortening her breath. She'd have to establish some quick ground rules, she told herself, anticipating the upcoming reunion.

"How much farther, Aunt Jane?"

"Just a little bit, scamp." She stopped, tuning out the insect noise and bird songs. "Listen, Mandy. Can you hear that gurgling water?"

Mandy closed her eyes, listening intently. Her green eyes popped open. "Yes, I hear it."

"That means we're almost there." Jane took her by the hand. "Come on. The house is just ahead."

They made quick work of the last few yards and burst through the fringe of underbrush. Jane pulled Amanda ahead of her so that the child could get a good first look at Nicolas Thunderheart's Eden.

Jane squatted down beside her niece. "Well? Isn't it wonderful?" she whispered, placing an arm around Mandy's waist.

"Oh, my!" Mandy's eyes rounded. "Is that where we'll be staying? In that house hanging over the water?"

"Yes." Jane gave her a squeeze. "It's better than a tree house, isn't it?"

Mandy giggled. "What keeps it from falling into the water?"

"It has huge supports under it. Once, it was a bridge—well, actually, a train trestle. But the railroad abandoned the route."

"Wow. This is way cool."

Jane laughed softly and hugged her niece again. "Wait until you see inside it. It's like living in a..." Her voice trailed off as her attention was captured by movement in the stream.

Nic waded into view. He stood in the stream, the water lapping at his muscled calves. He'd rolled his pant legs up to the knees. His gleaming torso was bare.

Holding a spear in one hand, he searched the sparkling water, poised, as alert as a wild animal on the prowl.

Mandy sucked in a breath and Jane quieted her with a finger to her lips. Still holding Mandy by the hand, Jane stood and moved forward with the child. Nicolas was so absorbed in watching the water that he didn't sense their silent approach. Jane and Mandy stopped in the shadows of the house.

Suddenly, Nic tensed and struck. The spear flashed and stabbed the water, then withdrew just as quickly to reveal a writhing, speckled trout at the end of it. Droplets of water flew in all directions, changing into tiny rainbows when struck by the sun. Nic waded toward the shore and removed the trout from the end of the long spear. He dropped his flopping prey into a basket. Jane caught sight of several other fish inside the wire cage before he lowered it back into the stream.

Jane gently pushed Mandy around the corner, out of sight, and bent to whisper in her ear, "Stay here. Let me talk to him first."

Mandy nodded, and Jane stepped from the shadows into a square of sunlight.

"Nicolas?"

He had started to turn back and wade into the stream, but her voice spun him around to her. His eyes widened and his mouth went slack. He blinked as if he couldn't believe she was real.

"Jane!" The joy in his voice and on his face brought a happy laugh from her. "What a surprise! How'd you...? Never mind that." He scrambled up the bank. Jane hurried forward and into his embrace.

His lips brushed her cheek, her forehead, and his arms felt like bands of security around her. He smelled manly and his skin tasted salty when she pressed her mouth against his shoulder. The pleasure she experienced in his arms made her wonder if her mission here was completely altruistic.

He drew back, his brows knitted. "You said you had plans for the holidays. Is something wrong? Did something happen I should know about?"

"A woman can change her mind, can't she?" Jane moved out of his embrace, mindful that Amanda was watching them. "Nothing's wrong, Nicolas, so stop worrying."

He smiled. "I'm glad you changed your mind. I wasn't looking forward to being alone during Thanksgiving. Usually, I don't sweat stuff like that, but this holiday...well, it was different."

Jane nodded, glancing over her shoulder. Amanda still hung back in the shadows.

"Jane, what's wrong?"

She faced him again and took a deep breath to steady her nerves. "Nic, all she knows is that you're my friend and we're visiting you over Thanksgiving. That's all she's going to know for now. We play by my rules or I take her back to Dallas."

Realization dawned on his face and he paled. *"You brought her?"*

"Yes. But you'll play by my rules?"

He nodded. "Whatever." Moving to one side, he looked around, his keen eyesight dissecting shadows, picking out the slightest movements.

Jane turned toward the house. "Amanda? Come here and meet my friend."

Mandy edged around the corner of the house and sprinted toward Jane, the breeze blowing at the curls of her dark hair, her backpack bumping against her scrawny shoulders. Smiling, Jane glanced toward Nic and her heart froze for a moment of sweet reflection.

Love painted Nic's face with softness and wonder. His eyes glowed with awe and his smile was so pure, so genuinely affectionate, that tears blurred Jane's vision. Swallowing a lump of emotion, Jane held out her hand to Mandy.

"Scamp, this is Nicolas Thunderheart. Nic, this is my favorite niece, Amanda."

Amanda tipped back her head to see Nic's face. "Hello. I like your house and I never saw anybody catch a fish like that before."

Nic knelt before her and placed a gentle hand on top of her baseball cap. "Amanda." He said her name as if it were a prayer or a magic word that would conjure up all things wondrous. When Amanda looked at Jane, clearly perplexed by his intense regard, Nic cleared his throat and stood straight, but his eyes glimmered with emotion.

"Sweet Lady Jane, I'll never be able to repay you," he said. "She's beautiful. She's...she has features like my mother and—"

"Nic, be good," Jane said sternly, glancing at Mandy and relieved to see that the basket of writhing fish at water's edge had her attention. "No more surprises. Mandy and I wanted to take a little trip and we thought this would be a great place to spend Thanksgiving. Her mother is visiting friends and left her in my care.''

"Ah." His brows dipped in a frown. "If she were *my* daughter, I would want to spend every holiday with her. What better time to be with your family than at Thanksgiving and Christmas?"

Jane shook her head, not liking the unfair comparison. "Selena is usually with Mandy at Thanksgiving. This is the first time she's been away."

"You know what? I went fishing once, but I used a pole and a hook," Mandy said, oblivious of the tension radiating between Jane and Nic.

Nic smiled at his daughter. "I use a fishing pole every so often, too. The trout were so thick this afternoon I decided I could spear them pretty easily." He bent lower to see her face under the bill of the ball cap. "So you're a Texas Rangers fan, I see."

Mandy glanced at Jane. "Me and Aunt Jane have season tickets."

"Are you going to give Mandy the deluxe tour of this place?"

"Where are my manners?" He turned Mandy around and removed her backpack. "Let me take this, then I'll show you my super-duper tree house."

"*Another* cool house?" Mandy asked with wide-eyed amazement, which won a laugh from Nic. "You live here by yourself and you have *two* houses?"

"Guess I'm just a man looking for the perfect nest." He placed a hand on Amanda's shoulder and then his eyes met Jane's. Gratitude welled in them, and she felt good all over. Seeing the twin expressions of happiness on Nic's and Mandy's faces, Jane's apprehension melted away. It was going to be a lovely Thanksgiving.

NIC WATCHED AS AMANDA splashed in the stream, wetting her jeans from the knees down. Laughing, she slapped the water, sending up sprays and rainbows.

"I like this place," she announced, tramping over to Nic and sitting on the bank beside him. She tipped back her head, giving her sweet face to the sun.

It was all Nic could do not to hug her to his chest and tell her that she was his and he'd never, ever let Selena keep her from him again. He glanced toward the house. No sign of Jane. She'd gone to unpack and take a couple of aspirin, maybe lie down for a few minutes to ease a headache. He had no doubt that her aching head was stress related. They were all stressed out. He looked at the child beside him, wondering how she would react when told he was her father. He'd agreed with Jane that he wouldn't . . . but he was damned tempted.

"Are there any kids around here?" Mandy asked, her green eyes meeting his.

"Sure, but they live a few miles away. There is a town nearby called Asheville. That's where the children here go to school. Do you like school?"

"Yes. My school is just two blocks from my house."

"That's nice." He couldn't get over how much she resembled his mother. Of course, he'd been told all his life that he, too, shared his mother's features. This child was his, no doubt, and she was the most beautiful creature in the world.

"Mommy says I might go to a different school after Christmas break, but I don't want to. It's a school where you have to live."

"A boarding school."

She nodded, her expression suddenly grave. "Mommy thinks it will be fun, but I don't know..." She kicked at a pebble. "I like school, but I don't want to live in it."

He rested a hand on top of her head. "I don't blame you. I wouldn't want to live in a school all the time, either. How would you like to live here?"

She looked around, sizing up the place. "It could be fun, but Mommy wouldn't like it. She doesn't like the outdoors."

He nodded, remembering vividly Selena's complaints if he even opened a window. She was allergic to fresh air, claimed it would ruin her "instrument."

"Your aunt likes it."

"She's like me. She loves animals and flowers. We like to smell the rain and roll in the grass." Mandy giggled and stretched out her short legs. She stared at the clouds, pointing out one. "Look, there's a pig." She fell back, lying flat. "See it? Not the whole pig. Just its head."

Nic lay beside her, cradling his head in one hand. He located the pig-shaped cloud. "Yes, I see it. The one beside it looks like a duck."

She giggled again. "That's not a duck! That's a cat. Its legs are too long to be a duck."

"You're right. I'm rusty. I haven't looked for cloud animals in a long time." He turned his head, giving in to the need to examine her every feature again, to admire the cap of shiny hair, the sweep of lashes, the scattering of freckles, the blush of rose in her cheeks. His daughter. His cute, fun, smart daughter, who loved the outdoors and could see barnyards in the sky. A vise squeezed his heart until tears collected in the corners of his eyes.

Damn Selena for keeping this treasure from him. But with the curse, came the guilt. He had said once that he wanted no children. But he wasn't the first man, or woman for that matter, to change his mind once his life had taken a different turn. He was ready for fatherhood now, firmly in his "seed" stage. Gritting his teeth, he bit back the confession that clamored in his throat.

"There you are," Jane said, striding toward them.

Aunt Jane to the rescue, Nicolas thought as Mandy sprang up and skipped toward Jane. How long did she expect him to keep quiet about being Mandy's father?

To his way of thinking, the sooner people were straight with Mandy, the better.

AFTER A FUN-FILLED DAY and a full stomach, Amanda fell asleep almost the moment her head hit the pillow. Standing beside one of the twin beds in the room she would share with her niece, Jane pushed Mandy's dark curls off her forehead. She was a beautiful child.

Mandy and Nic had gotten along great. Becoming his shadow, Mandy had gone with him to the tree house, then had explored the outbuildings. She'd helped him prepare their dinner of broiled trout, steamed vegetables and freshly baked zucchini bread. Jane had gotten a kick out of watching them enjoy each other. Mandy had laughed at Nic's corny jokes, and he had hung on Mandy's every word, every giggle, every smile. He was the epitome of the doting daddy.

Giving Mandy a soft kiss on her forehead, Jane straightened and joined Nic again in the living room. He sat in one of the big easy chairs, his bare feet propped on the rustic coffee table, a book open in his lap. Seeing her, he removed his wire-framed reading glasses and set them and the book aside.

Longing curled in the pit of Jane's stomach, making her tremble. His dark hair fell in an attractive disarray across his forehead and the tips of his ears. He wore black jeans and a gray T-shirt, and she had never seen a more sexy-looking man in all her life.

"Is she all tucked in?"

"Yes, she's a very tired little girl." She moved closer, each step increasing her longing for him. "Well, what do you think?"

"She's beautiful, of course. She looks like me." He grinned devilishly. "Seriously, I'm proud to be her father. Damned proud. I'd like to climb to the highest peak and yell it to the world."

"Which brings me to the ground rules." She sat on the sofa.

"Same here."

"Nicolas, Selena doesn't know I've brought Mandy here."

He rubbed a hand up and down his face, then around to the back of his neck. "I figured as much."

Jane sat on the couch. "I've gone behind Selena's back again. Don't make me sorry that I did."

"You couldn't convince her that I was a fit father, I take it."

"She thinks you have ulterior motives."

"Such as?"

"Turning Mandy against her."

He fell back in the chair. "What a crock! Even *she* can't believe that. Why would I do such a thing? I don't hate Selena. I just don't want to be around her."

"Why?"

"Because she reminds me of what I used to be and of a way of life I've put behind me."

"I think Selena will come around given some time. I need that time, Nic. I don't want her to know about this visit until *I* tell her about it."

"And when are you going to do that? I don't like this sneaking around, Jane." He jabbed a thumb at his chest. "I have rights, you know."

"Yes, I know, but I don't want you telling Mandy that you're her father until I say it's okay. She's a kid. I don't want her messed up over this."

"How would that mess her up? I would think that she'd want a father."

"We need to ease her into this. Please?"

"Are you regretting your decision to bring her here?"

"No." She curled her legs up onto the couch and looked out at the trees swaying gracefully against the night sky. "Every little girl should have a daddy who loves her and adores being with her."

He tented his fingers in front of his face and regarded her steadily over the tips of them. "I'd like for you to tell me about it. Tell me about your problems with your father. Maybe it will help me understand why you think I should keep my mouth shut about how much I love the fact that Mandy's mine."

"This isn't about me or what happened when I was a girl."

"Let me be the judge of that." He smiled, encouraging her to open up. "Tell me, Jane. I'm listening."

She screwed up her courage and let herself speak of her most painful regrets and disappointments. "Okay. You asked for it." Plucking restlessly at the fringe of a wool throw draped across the back of the sofa, she conjured up those dark days of her youth.

"For years I was convinced that my mother was keeping me from my father, like Selena has kept you away from Amanda. I couldn't allow myself to believe that my father wouldn't want to see me. That was too awful to contemplate. I mean, I was a lovable kid." She forced a smile. "Who wouldn't love me?"

"You bet," Nicolas agreed with a tender smile.

"When I was approaching my fourteenth birthday I had a big argument with my mother and I accused her of lying to me about my father. He paid child support, so he must want to be involved in my life. Mother said that he hadn't paid child support since he'd remarried, which had been five or six years before then. She finally relented and gave me his phone number. I called." Jane took a deep breath, the memory of that telephone conversation still packing a punch.

Nic propped his feet on the coffee table again and waited, his fingers still tented, his eyes still probing.

"I got him on the phone and he sounded uncomfortable. I did most of the talking at first. I guess he was tongue-tied. Finally, he broke in and asked what I wanted." She managed a mirthless laugh. "I told him I just wanted to talk to him. I wanted to get to know him, if possible."

Jane linked her fingers tightly in her lap and stared stonily at the twinkling stars visible through the tree branches. The torment of that long-ago conversation stung her and she erected the shields around her heart again.

"He had a new family, he told me. A son and two other daughters that were his whole world. They didn't even know about me, and he thought it was best if we kept it that way." She was amazed that she could keep her tone so even, almost casual. "I told him that I was his child, too. He repeated that he had a new family now." She smiled grimly. "I got the message. He was, in effect, saying, 'Go away, kid. You bother me.'" Giving a faint shrug, she looked at Nicolas. His expression was troubled, his eyes shimmering with sympathy.

"You never spoke to him again?" His voice sounded strained and hoarse.

"No. Once was enough. Rejection, I can live without." She looked away from him. His sharing of her pain brought a lump to her throat. He was obviously upset by her story, and that made her want to crawl into his embrace and accept the comforting words she knew he wanted to give her.

"So you didn't believe Selena when she fed you that bull about how I didn't want a child?" A smile touched one corner of his mouth. "You still believe there are men who want their children—*all* of their offspring?"

"I believe that, but I also believed Selena. However, I know people can change their minds. I thought you might have reconsidered and that you'd want your daughter now. If there was a chance, I wanted to give it to Mandy. I know I have this chunk missing from me. In here," she said, tapping a fist between her breasts. "My father's love could have filled it. Every daughter should have her father's love first before any other man's."

"So why shouldn't I tell Mandy that she's mine?"

"I want to have Selena's permission."

Nicolas left the chair and sat next to her on the couch. "I want to roll back time so I can know Mandy from the day she was born, but that's asking for miracles. You're asking for miracles, too."

"Maybe. I need time, Nic. My relationship with my sister just might be at stake here."

He opened his arms to her. Jane hesitated only a moment before snuggling against him. He was quiet for several minutes and so was she.

"Weird," he whispered.

"What's weird?"

"Your father's reaction. Out of sight, out of mind." His voice was low and purring. "But how can a parent forget his own child? Just because he remarried and fathered other children? Doesn't make sense to me, but I can't say this is the first time I've heard of this. People get divorced and one parent gets custody of the children and the other walks off and never looks back. Doesn't even provide financial support."

"Yeah, and I thought he'd been making those payments. Mother had let me go on believing. She hated that he had completely turned his back on me."

"Selena's father stayed in the picture, though."

"Yes. He was always around. He doted on Selena."

"Did he ever remarry?"

"Yes, and he has a stepson with his second wife, but he never missed his weekend visits with Selena. And he also paid his child support."

"Which made it all the more worse for you," Nic added, his arms tightening around her. "Being a parent isn't something that's inbred. When my brother needed me, I wasn't there for him, and I'll never forgive myself for that. I should have stepped up to the plate, but I balked."

"Nicolas, you did your best."

"No, I didn't. I was selfish as hell and didn't want to give my brother any of my precious time. My business, my social engagements, Selena, all came before my brother. Shouldn't have been that way."

"But you learned your lesson. I can already see that you will be a good father to Mandy. I bet your brother understands that you just weren't emotionally prepared to handle him at that time."

"Yes, he understands. We're close now, but he'll never be as close to me as he is to our uncle." He released a long breath. "Ah, well. What's done is done."

"Maybe this is your second chance—to make it right."

"Yes, my second chance. Want me to show you how grateful I am to you for having a hand in that?"

Laughing, she sat up. "Don't tempt me."

"Where are you going?" he asked with a down-fallen expression.

"To sleep." Before he could persuade her other-wise, Jane stood and moved toward the archway that led to the bedrooms. "See you in the morning."

"Spoilsport," he groused, but reached for his book and reading glasses again. "Hey, Jane."

"Yes?" She paused on the threshold.

"I'm glad you told me about your father."

She smiled, thinking he was the most wonderful man and would certainly make a most wonderful mate. "So am I, Nicolas. G'night."

Chapter Ten

Puttering happily in the kitchen, Jane decided she could easily get used to living in Nic's house. After a huge Thanksgiving feast, complete with the best mincemeat pie she'd ever put in her mouth, Jane had insisted on cleaning the dishes, as Nic had slaved in the kitchen since sunrise. She smiled, remembering how she'd found him this morning. Rising at around eight, she wasn't surprised to find that he had been up for hours. His bubbling excitement at having her and Mandy as his Thanksgiving guests was infectious.

The kitchen had already smelled of roasting turkey and savory dressing. Nic, wearing a flour-smudged apron, had been rolling out dumpling and pie dough and he'd greeted her with a beatific smile and smacking kiss, then he'd shoved a cup of coffee and a carrot muffin at her and had told her to relax because he had everything under control.

"What a man," she breathed as she stacked the clean pots and pans on the stove for him to return to their proper places later.

She strolled to the bank of windows in the living area, but she couldn't see Nicolas or Amanda. They'd gone on a nature walk after supper at Jane's insistence. She wanted to give them time alone together. Her intentions hadn't gone unnoticed by Nic. He'd mouthed a thank-you before he'd set off with Mandy into the forest that was now a riot of autumn colors.

They should be returning soon, she thought with a glance at the sky. It would be getting dark in another hour.

Mandy already thought Nic was a wonder. Jane laughed to herself, recalling when her niece had commented that she'd never known that men could cook before. Jane had detected admiration and the beginnings of hero worship in that statement. Perhaps, when it was time for Mandy to know that Nicolas Thunderheart was her father, the transition wouldn't be a rocky one. If Mandy and Nic continued to forge a strong friendship, then the next step wouldn't be traumatic.

Maybe he was right. Maybe she was worrying for nothing. There was a good chance that Mandy would be thrilled to discover that Nic was her father. But that revelation would change a lot of things, Jane knew. Some for the better, some not. She determined to go slow, to be cautious.

Hearing a jaunty whistle, she blinked and focused her eyes again to see Mandy and Nic walking toward the house. Seeing Jane standing by the windows, he raised a hand in greeting. She waved back. Mandy raced ahead, and Jane heard the door open downstairs, followed by the pounding of Mandy's feet.

"Aunt Jane, Aunt Jane! We saw a deer and her baby!" Mandy's voice raced her upstairs and won. "It looked just like Bambi."

"I bet it was pretty," Jane said, reaching out to give her niece a hug. She helped Mandy out of her sweater. "What else did you see?"

"Eagles and hawks." Mandy pushed her damp bangs off her forehead. "And tracks—fox, squirrel and coyote tracks. Nic showed me how to tell them apart."

"That's always good to know," Jane said, partly teasing as she looked to Nic, who'd come upstairs. Black jeans and green plaid, wool shirt looked wonderful on him.

"It smells like winter out there," he said. "You know, that sharp smell that usually precedes snow."

"Snow? It's going to snow?"

"Not today or tonight, but soon." He went to the fireplace and fed a few more sticks of wood to the cracking flames. "I love winter here."

"You love every season here," Jane said.

He nodded and glanced over his shoulder at her. "Wouldn't you?"

"Yes," she answered simply, truthfully. Every season would hold its own magic in these woods.

Mandy yawned, and Jane noticed her drooping eyelids.

"Hey, I think you need a bath before you get ready for bed," Jane said. "Maybe you could sweet-talk Nic into hauling in some water."

"I don't want a bath." She made a face. "I'm not dirty."

"Oh, no?" Jane caught Mandy by the wrists and examined her grubby hands. "Look at this, will you? If that's not dirt, then it's rust and you're in worse shape than I thought."

Nic laughed and ran a hand over Mandy's tousled hair. "I'll take a bath if you will, funny face," he told the child. "Come on. You can help me draw the water and heat it."

Mandy followed him, trotting to keep up with his long-legged stride. Jane settled back in an easy chair with a smile. If Selena could only see Nic and Mandy together, even she would have to admit that they would be good for each other.

As soon as she returned to Texas, she'd have to tell Selena what she'd done, Jane thought nervously. But once her sister stopped yelling and pouting, Jane was certain she could make her listen to reason. They'd take it one step at a time.

JANE SNUGGLED into a pink chenille robe, then checked on Mandy. She was fast asleep, her small body a mere bump under the bed linens and blankets. Tiptoeing from the room, she closed the door softly behind her, then went into the living room.

Nic crouched in front of the fireplace and jabbed at the burning logs with a poker. He had slipped into a pair of loose jeans and a T-shirt after his bath, leaving his feet bare and his hair damp and in attractive disarray. He grinned at her.

"You look cute in that robe."

She settled on the couch to admire the night outside the windows. The full moon gave enough light for her to see the outbuildings and bird feeders. Moon glow changed the stream into a fluttering ribbon of silver and gold.

"Mandy's asleep," she said. "She had a good time today."

"So did I." He sat beside her and slid an arm around her shoulders. It felt as right as rain. Propping his feet on the coffee table, he released a contented sigh. "Best Thanksgiving I can remember."

She smiled. "Me, too."

He cocked an eyebrow. "No kidding?"

"No kidding." She settled more comfortably against him. "I dread going back to work."

"You don't like your work?"

"Oh, I like it. I'll just have trouble keeping my mind on jewelry designs. I'll be thinking about this place and you and how I'm going to break the news to Selena." She glanced sharply at him. "You're not going to send another fax, are you?"

He widened his eyes, feigning innocence. "What? Me? No way!"

"You'd better be a good boy. I've placed my relationship with my sister on the line for you." Turning sideways, she rested her cheek on his shoulder and spread one hand against his chest. He was solid, but his beating heart reminded her that he was also soft and vulnerable in certain places. "Can I ask you something about your past?"

"Fire away."

"What happened with Prescott?"

He released a sighing groan. "Not that. I thought you were going to ask about my marriage or divorce. You really want to know about Prescott?"

"I can't figure it out. He must have pulled the wool over your eyes, but you're so smart, I can't understand why you couldn't see it coming."

"I didn't see it coming because I wasn't looking. When it came to Barrett Prescott, I trusted him completely. There was no reason for me to keep an eye on him."

"So what happened?" she urged. "Look, I can understand that you don't want to talk about it, but I want to know. I tried to follow the scandal through newspapers and magazines. I wasn't in the country then and the reports were sketchy."

"Surely your family told you all you wanted to know."

"Selena was closemouthed about it. She said it was business mumbo jumbo that she didn't understand."

"Well, that's true. Selena never wanted to understand my business. Any time I started to talk about my work, her eyes glazed over."

Jane giggled, having seen that particular expression on Selena's face many times before. "She does the same thing when I talk about my jewelry."

He placed a hand over hers resting against his chest. "I want to see some of your designs. I bet they're beautiful."

"They are, but back to Prescott," she insisted, forcing him back to the subject. "What made him do what he did? I mean, dumping medical refuse in the ocean. It's so completely against everything you and Prescott preached. I remember when I read the first news reports, I didn't believe a word of it. It was ludicrous."

"And what made you change your mind?"

She furrowed her brow, thinking back. "Prescott's confession is what did it. That shattered my faith."

"Mine, too."

Jane rubbed her cheek against his shirt. "So tell me what happened and how you were duped so that you can get back on that white charger where you belong."

He was quiet for a few moments, his heartbeats filling her head. "No one is completely innocent and I don't belong on a white charger, but I'll tell you what happened." He caressed her arm, his fingers moving up and down on the nubby chenille material. "Barrett made a few bad investments and he was bailed out by some ruthless men. I didn't know anything about this at the time. Barrett was good at keeping up a happy, successful front. I could tell him anything, and I thought the feeling was mutual, but I overestimated the friendship."

"Ruthless men as in the Mafia?" Jane asked.

"I don't know about that. They were greedy and didn't give a damn about their fellow man. They decided to use Barrett's shipping line to get rid of medical wastes by dumping them in the ocean. Barrett went along because they had him by the short hairs. He owed them more money than he could ever repay."

"This illegal activity would cancel that debt?"

"Yes, that was the deal."

"Sounds to me like Prescott wasn't as dedicated to his principles as you are."

"Being successful—or rather the *appearance* of success—was all-important to Barrett. He loved living in a huge house, wearing Armani suits, diamond pinky rings and Italian-made shoes. He got a big kick out of picking up the tab, buying his own private jet, throwing parties for the elite. All that jazz bores the stuffing out of me.''

"Me, too," she said, smiling. "If you weren't into all the trappings, what joy did you get out of it?''

"The work, of course," he said matter-of-factly. "Believing that we were setting an example, blazing a trail for others to follow. In those days ethical investments were a pioneering form of business. I was hopeful that we would beef up the conscience of the business world and shame others into taking a closer look at how and what they were supporting.''

"You did make a difference, Nicolas."

"Yes, but the scandal destroyed everything I'd worked so hard for. The first inkling I had was when a reporter called and told me that she was doing investigative work on Barrett and that she'd uncovered some troubling things. She asked me what I knew about Corningwall Shipping. That was the shipping firm Barrett had bought stock in, then had convinced me to do the same. He supported the company, so I knew it was on the up-and-up. I told the reporter I had every faith in it." He laughed bitterly. "Bad mistake.''

She stroked her hand over his chest and down to his flat stomach, sensing the mounting agitation in him.

"Other rumblings reached me until I finally asked Barrett why there was a buzz around the shipping line. He downplayed the whole thing and said it was a case of ambitious reporters trying to tear down all the good work we'd done. That didn't exactly jive with me, and for the first time since I'd met him, I didn't entirely believe his story. I did some checking on my own, but I was too late. The story broke and I had egg all over my face.''

''Did Barrett confess then?''

''Not at first, and when he did, he told it to the law instead of to me. I was one of the last to discover that our reputation was in the gutter and that Barrett had sold us out. Corningwall was dumping toxic and medical wastes, all kinds of garbage, into the environment.''

''But your name was eventually cleared.''

''Yes. They had nothing on me. Barrett actually admitted I was in the dark. But I still came off looking like a dumb second banana. He was the Skipper and I was Gilligan and I woke up in a new world every damn morning. That's how it looked, and for a long time that's how I felt.''

''Once again, you were way too hard on yourself.''

''I've never been that low and I don't want to ever be that down again.'' He ran a hand through his hair, which was nearly dry now. ''I look back on it and I see all the mistakes and marvel at how stupid I was. I sacrificed everything for my work—my marriage, integrity, my own brother when he needed me the most. Hell, I didn't even grieve that much when my parents died. I was too preoccupied with being the golden boy of the business world. I put everything I was into one basket and when it overturned, I had nothing left.''

''Except yourself,'' Jane noted. ''And everything wonderful that you are.'' She raised up to look into his eyes. ''Nicolas, look what you've accomplished since then. Maybe that awful scandal was necessary to bring you to this place in your life."

"Yes, I've thought of that, too. I probably would have grown tired of the eighteen-hour days, the hassles, the headaches, and chucked the whole lot myself after a few years. What hurt most was the realization that all my personal investments had been bad ones. I might have been a whiz kid at business investments, but I was a colossal failure as a human being."

"Nic," Jane scolded softly, then dropped a kiss on his lips. "You made a few mistakes and you trusted the wrong people. That doesn't make you the fool of the world." She rested her mouth lightly on his again. "I've placed you back on that white charger, my shining knight."

He smiled against her lips. "You're nothing if not persistent. I told you, the suit of armor doesn't fit. Never did."

"It does in *my* fantasy."

Angling a look at her, he studied her. "Just where did you ever get the idea that I was knight material, anyway? Did Selena ever wax poetic about me?"

"Oh, she did at first, but I didn't pay that much attention. After you two were married, I was curious about my new brother-in-law and I started noticing your name cropping up in news reports. You have to understand I was eighteen or nineteen back then and, typical of that age, I was passionate about changing the world."

"Ah, it begins to become clear," he said with a smile. "You saw me as a crusader."

ashed through her mind. Like Tarzan

u smiling at?'' he asked, setting her on
pping his hands from her shoulders all
o her hips.

er fingers up the front of his T-shirt.
e wicked images skipping through my

nds interesting.'' He kissed her waiting
e I'm the star attraction.''
e definitely the leading man.'' She moved
m to take in her surroundings. His bed
vith mosquito netting, and a skylight
ved a circle of starry night. He pushed
ng and flicked back the white-fur skin he
read. The sheet beneath was ebony, the
ith crimson. Sexy.
a deep, quivery breath. ''Suddenly, I'm all
gs.'' She looked across the bed at him.
it you? Having second thoughts?''
his T-shirt up and over his head, then flung
room. ''Not a chance, Lady Jane.''
th went dry and her heart lodged in her
chest was bronze with a light dusting of hair
r and in a straight line that disappeared into
vaistband. ''You look like a dream, Mr.
eart.''
ou, Ms. Litton, are a vision.'' He sat on the
eld out a hand to her. ''Don't be nervous.''
ghed, a high, fluty sound that sent flags of
er cheeks. But she sat on the firm bed and

''Definitely. I wanted to save the world. I protested anything nuclear or atomic or polluting. I saw all businesses as the enemy, but then you showed me that businessmen had consciences, too. I was thrilled to have you in the family, and many of my friends were impressed. I was kind of a minicelebrity until . . . well, the tide turned.''

''And you learned that you have to be careful which coattails you grab on to.''

''Yes, I guess so.'' She laughed, remembering her ideology back then. ''I hadn't thought about it that way until now, but I suppose some of my fury at you must have stemmed from no longer being envied by my friends. And I told you I had a huge crush on you. Selena thought that was hysterical.''

''Why?''

''Because she and I never had the same tastes in anything.''

''You mean, this Jerome guy doesn't float your boat?''

''Jerome?'' she squeaked. ''No way.'' She looked at him and found that he was smiling. Her heart skipped a beat as she recalled the many fantasies his smile had created back when she was a coed in England. ''I swear, sometimes I thought more of you than Selena did. When the scandal broke, I didn't believe a word of it at first, but Selena—'' She broke off that revelation, afraid she might reveal something too painful for Nicolas.

His smile became grim. ''I know. She didn't give me the benefit of the doubt. By then our marriage was crumbling and she blamed my obsession with my work.

When the quality of my work was questioned, Selena felt vindicated."

Regretting the sadness lurking in his eyes, Jane pressed a kiss to his cheek. Freshly shaven, his skin was smooth and the aroma of lime drifted to her. Mmm. He smelled good enough to eat. "I'm sorry for dredging up all this. You've worked hard to get past it."

"Yes, I have. And I am . . . past it."

"I can see that. I'm proud of you."

"Tell that to Selena. Maybe she will reconsider her stand that Mandy and I should remain strangers."

"You've done a good job of letting go of the past, but Selena is still holding on to some bitterness, I'm afraid. She doesn't like to fail, and the divorce is a big black mark for a perfectionist like her."

"I understand." He ran a hand over her hair. "You're between the proverbial rock and a hard place, aren't you?"

"Exactly, but I'm confident the future will be better for all of us."

He cradled her chin in his hand and kissed her forehead, the bridge of her nose, her eyelids. "We're all lucky to have you." He looked deeply into her eyes. Desire flamed in his. "Have you thought any about us?"

"Only every other minute of the day," she confessed. "We're a sticky wicket, wouldn't you agree?"

"Damned if we do, damned if we don't."

"Exactly."

"I wish we could have met under different circumstances. I would have poured on the charm and swept you off your feet."

"I must
dream in tha

"Oh, yeah
means, let me
exists."

She grabbed
need the outfit,
heart hammerin

His slow, cun
in her stomach.
now is touch me,

Blunt-ended fi
hair, and Jane me
lief. His mouth fla
plucking kisses tha
She drove her hand
warm, taut skin. Shu
warning her that a
would complicate an
breathed his name a
hers.

"We're probably cra

"I don't give a damn
into his arms. "We'd b
It's what we both want.

"Yes," she agreed, h
and across his wide shou

He carried her to his r
behind them. For all her
had to admit that she love
into his boudoir. Just li
thought, thrilling at the

from a movie fl
and Jane!

"What are yo
her feet and sli
the way down t

She walked

"Oh, at all th
mind."

"Umm, sou
mouth. "I ho

"Oh, you're
away from hi
was draped
above it sho
aside the nett
used as a sp
edges lined

Jane took
nerve endin

"What abo
He swept
it across the

Her mou
throat. His
in the cente
his jeans
Thunderh

"And y
bed and h

She lau
color to

placed her hand in his. "I don't want to give you the impression that I'm as green as a new sprout, but I have to admit it's been—"

He placed a finger to her lips. "I don't care," he told her, his eyes a dark jungle green. "Tonight, there have been no others. Only us." He kissed her lips lightly. Then he stood and went to the door. The sound of the lock falling into place sent a shiver of anticipation through Jane.

Nic sat on the bed again, hooked one hand on the robe's belt and pulled Jane against him. His mouth flirted with hers. Hers flirted back. He untied the belt and eased his hands inside to cup her breasts through the thin fabric of her nightgown.

She rained feverish kisses across his face and trembled when he licked a line up her neck. Somehow, her hand landed on his fly. She pushed the metal disk through the buttonhole. Her fingertips brushed across a hard bulge and something wild and wanton howled deep inside her.

The zipper on his jeans seemed to slide down by itself, or perhaps it was nudged open by what it tried to contain. His hands on her shoulders pressed her back to lie on the black linens that smelled like sunshine. He stood beside the bed and stripped off the rest of his clothes. Jane wondered if he knew how the sight of him made her insides heat and melt. He rested one knee on the firm mattress, but then stopped to gaze at her.

"God, you're beautiful."

Jane felt a warm blush wash over her face. She glanced down to see what had arrested his attention.

Her robe lay open, revealing her white lacy gown through which her pink nipples could be viewed.

"Beautiful," he whispered again.

"Stop," she pleaded, crossing her arms over her breasts. "You're embarrassing me, and I don't want to think. I only want to feel."

He smiled and nodded, then opened the top drawer of the bedside table.

Jane closed her eyes on a sigh of gratitude. It was so like him to assuage any fear or doubt, to make sure he'd done whatever he could to create a safe environment for their lovemaking.

Covering her body with his, Nic combed her hair back with gentle fingers. She kissed the curve of his jawline, loving the feel of his skin on hers, the caress of his cheek against her, the searing ardor of his mouth on hers. Her breasts ached and a heaviness invaded the lower part of her body. His tongue mated with hers and his clever fingers manipulated her nipples to hard, throbbing peaks.

Moaning his name, Jane stroked his back and shoulders, then kneaded the hard muscles of his buttocks. She could feel him between her thighs and she wanted him inside her, inside where she was on fire.

She raised up to shrug out of the robe. He eased her nightgown off her shoulders, down over her breasts and stomach. He dropped kisses on her thighs as he swept the garment off her legs and feet. Her nudity was revealed to him, and he seemed ever so pleased. When he kissed her again, there was a savagery there, an exciting impatience. She felt him between her thighs and her passion leapt like a flame.

"It's been awhile," he whispered hotly in her ear. "And I'm afraid my restraint isn't what it used to be."

"Don't hold back," she whispered.

"Thank God."

He brought one of her breasts up and into the warm, slick cavern of his mouth, then she felt him breach her. He took his time, letting her body adjust to the sweet intrusion of him. He was big, but her body opened for him, hungered for him. Jane shuddered, brought to a trembling climax by his flicking tongue on her sensitive breasts.

"Good, good," he murmured, kissing one stiff nipple. "Let yourself go."

She clutched at his hips as he orchestrated another shattering climax, which he shared with her. Chanting her name hoarsely, he threw back his head and rode his release all out, displaying not a drop of insecurity or self-consciousness.

Jane took added pleasure from watching the play of intense emotion on his face. His arms trembled, cords strained in his neck as he bared his teeth and rasped out words that were not for polite company, but added to the erotic thrill of the experience for her.

She heard her own ragged breathing and felt beads of perspiration on her body. Her heart galloped in her chest and her limbs trembled with the aftershocks of her own shattering release.

Nic bestowed lazy kisses on her parted lips and eased his rangy body off to one side of hers. He stroked her stomach and the undersides of her breasts.

"Are you okay?"

Jane laughed weakly. "You have to ask?"

"I mean, I didn't hurt you, did I?"

"You didn't hurt me," she assured him, turning to her side to face him. "But I probably won't be any good for any other man after that." She smiled at his look of confusion. "Once you've had the best..." She let him fill in the rest.

"Oh, yes," he agreed with a big grin. "I bet you say that to all the boys."

She kissed him and slid one hand down his furry stomach. "You make love like a wild man."

"You ain't seen nothing yet," he promised, removing the thin shield covering him before he pressed her back to the mattress and kissed her with renewed intensity. "Reach in that drawer for reinforcements, why don't you."

Jane widened her eyes. "Are you serious?"

"Oh, I'm *very* serious."

Amused and impressed with his fortitude, she did her best not to laugh. "Nicolas, take it easy or I'll be asking if *I* hurt *you*."

He regarded her with a half-serious expression. "Now I thought you'd learned your lesson the last time you lost faith in me. You're not doubting me again, are you?"

"Oookay," she said, drawing out the word as she reached into the drawer and felt a number of foil rectangles. She grabbed them all and dropped them on the bed. She counted six. "I'll just leave them right there so we won't have to fish them out of that drawer all night long."

Trepidation enlarged his green eyes and his mouth fell open. "Uh-oh. I think I'm sliding off that damned white horse again."

Laughing, Jane wrapped her limbs around him and kissed his smiling lips. "Don't worry. I'll cushion your fall."

Chapter Eleven

Stepping out of the shower, Jane listened intently but could no longer hear Mandy's happy laughter or Nic's deep chuckle downstairs.

She toweled off and sprinkled herself with jasmine-scented dusting powder before slipping into matching bra and panties of peachy lace and silk. Having left Nic and Mandy to clean up the breakfast dishes while she took a bath, Jane was glad for the window of time to be alone with her thoughts.

Trying to hold on to all the good aspects of last night, she smiled as she dressed in green corduroy slacks and a cream-colored, lightweight sweater with an olive houndstooth design. But for all the wonderful revelations that occurred last night between them, there were also a number of niggling worries harping at Jane. She stood by the window in the bedroom she was supposed to share with Mandy and glanced guiltily at her unslept-in bed.

"I might be asking for more trouble than I can handle," she whispered. For one thing, her family would be appalled at her for taking up with her sister's ex-husband. What was weird was that Jane had a hard time even thinking of him in such terms. It seemed totally improbable that this man had once been married to her sister.

Selena would definitely see this as consorting with the enemy, and her sister was still stinging from the earlier betrayal of confidence. Jane knew she'd once again gambled with the relationship by bringing Mandy to meet her father, but now that she and Nic had slept together . . . well, that changed the whole equation. She'd probably place Mandy in that boarding school with instructions that Aunt Jane was *never, ever* allowed near her.

"And who could blame her?" Jane mumbled, staring sightlessly outside where the sun was reaching its zenith in a robin's-egg blue sky. Closing her eyes, she leaned her forehead against the cool glass pane. "But none of that bothers me as much as what he said . . ."

Her thoughts scurried back to last night when she had snuggled in his arms with sleep only minutes away. Why had he said that? she wondered with an inner moan as his voice drifted back to her and his words fell like stones against her heart.

"I'll never be able to repay you for what you've done, Jane," he'd whispered, his lips stroking her cheek. "Thank you for bringing Mandy to me. I hope that tonight has shown you how much this all means to me."

Wincing, Jane wrenched her mind from that memory. She should have confronted him right then and demanded if his lovemaking had been an act of gratitude instead of mindless passion. Damn it, she wanted mindless passion. He could take his gratitude and shove it.

She certainly couldn't trust his feelings for her until he could convince her that his reasons for wanting to be with her last night had nothing to do with Mandy.

"Aunt Jane?"

Jane turned to find Mandy standing just inside the room. Her eyelids were droopy. "Uh-oh. Somebody looks sleepy. Getting up so early tuckers you out, doesn't it?"

"I guess." Mandy rubbed her eyes. "We cleaned up the kitchen and Nic read me a story." She yawned and kicked off her shoes. "And I got sleepy."

"So I see." Jane pulled the bedspread down on the bed Mandy used. "So hop in. A nap will do you good. When you wake up maybe Nic will take us pinecone hunting."

"Okay. That'll be fun. What can we do with pinecones?"

"Oh, we can decorate them, burn them in the fireplace. All sorts of things." She pulled the spread up over Mandy and kissed her cheek. "Sweet dreams, scamp."

"I like Nic, Aunt Jane. He's real smart. He knows all about flowers and animals and..." She paused to yawn again. "And stuff like that."

Jane smiled and closed the bedroom door, leaving her niece to her dreams. She found Nic in the library where he was replacing a book on the shelves. He smiled warmly at her and Jane questioned how she could have ever thought any other man's smile attractive.

"Mandy's in for a nap."

"Yes, she was half-asleep when I finished our story."

Jane paused to admire the sight of him in jeans and a red sweater with the Smokies behind him, ablaze with gold and orange. "Will you look at that view? I can't get over how beautiful it is here."

"We shouldn't be wasting our time inside. Let's go to the tree house."

Jane glanced toward the archway, which gave access to the hallway and bedrooms, but Nic caught one of her hands.

"You put Amanda down for a nap, didn't you?"

"Yes."

"Then she'll be fine. Come on." He pulled her into the curve of his arm. "The last time I was in that tree house with you, I kissed you and lost it."

"Lost what?"

"Any hope of keeping you at a safe distance." He grinned and placed a tender kiss on her forehead. "This time, I'll probably lose my heart."

Jane closed her eyes, knowing she'd already lost hers.

They left the house, hand in hand. The air was crisp with autumn and redolent with wood smoke. Jane followed behind Nic up the tree and looped her arms around his neck for a ride to the top floor. When her feet left the platform, she gave a little laugh and he kissed her, his mouth moving over hers in a stirring, searching communion. She clung to him, her body throbbing for his, her senses reeling as she flew up, up through leaves and branches. He held onto the rope with one hand, his other arm wrapped tightly about her waist.

"Touchdown," he murmured against her lips as their feet found the top platform. "What a ride." He stepped out of the rope loop and gathered her in his arms again. He kissed her hard, his tongue plundering her mouth, his hands on her hips, drawing her against him.

Jane broke the kiss first and wiggled from his arms. She turned her back on him to admire the view and control her rioting emotions. He slipped his arms around her from behind.

"What's wrong?" he asked.

"I'm wondering where we go from here," she said. "Should I tell Selena what's happened between us?"

"Why not?"

"Oh, I can think of a couple dozen reasons. First and foremost, you used to be married to her. Don't you think it's a tad uncomfortable to be sleeping with her sister now?"

"Are you uncomfortable with it?"

"I asked you first," she hedged.

"To be honest, I don't think of you as Selena's sister. You're you. Period."

"But I *am* her sister and I used to be your sister-in-law."

"Yes, but I didn't know anything about you then. Does this really bug you?"

"No, but it should."

"Why borrow trouble?"

"True. We have enough trouble as it is."

"I think what happened between us last night eliminates trouble instead of creating it."

"How's that?"

"We're in sync now. We want the same things."

She rested her head back against his shoulder. "That's partly true."

"Partly?"

"Selena is family, Nic. She's been a terrific mother to Mandy, and I would never do anything to jeopardize that."

"But you agree that I should be included in Amanda's life."

"Yes, but I have to think of Selena's feelings first. She has to agree. I don't want to hurt her any more than I already have."

"Neither do I, but I have a right to be with Amanda." His tone was hard and his arms weren't as welcoming. She could feel the tension in him.

"Of course." She sighed. "But we have to go slow, Nic. I feel your impatience. You have a lot of ground to cover, a lot of years to make up for, but we have to be careful not to ruin a good thing." She summoned her courage and told herself she had to know his motives for last night or she'd always wonder. "What happened between us last night has nothing to do with Mandy, does it?"

"With Mandy?" He sounded puzzled.

"You said you were grateful," she reminded him. "I want to be square with you, Nic. What happened between us doesn't change my mind or my stand. I'll do what I think is best for Mandy."

Gripping her shoulders, he turned her around to face him. A hint of anger blazed in his eyes. "You think last night was a ploy by me to get in your good graces? You think I made love to you out of gratitude?"

She shrugged. "You said something to that effect."

"I don't remember what I said, but that's not what I meant. I made love to you last night because I couldn't stop myself. I wanted you then as I want you now, and it has nothing to do with Mandy or gratitude." He spread his hands on either side of her head and tipped her face up until he could look down into her eyes. "I feel as if I've waited my whole life for you, Jane."

Her heart swelled. "Did you feel this way about Selena?"

He frowned. "That was a long time ago."

"I want to know. Tell me."

"We were too young and too self-involved back then. We should have had an affair instead of marrying, but we let our hormones lead us to Las Vegas and a wedding chapel. Two months later, we were already arguing and doubting what we felt for each other. Selena has told you this, I'm sure."

"Yes, but I need to hear it from you. You don't harbor any feelings for her? You loved her enough to marry her, so those emotions might be all mixed up with what you feel about me."

He rocked his head backward and laughed. "No way, lady. You and Selena are like night and day. Besides, I'm not the same man who married your sister. I've grown so much since then, and I have a different outlook on life and completely different priorities. The man I was back then wouldn't have been good enough for you."

She curved her hands at his neck, her thumbs sliding along his clean-shaven jawline. "This feels right. Last night seemed like a destiny fulfilled."

"I agree. If it's not destiny, then it's magic, and either way, it's the most wonderful thing in my life right now."

The confession sent her heart soaring and the world seemed brighter and full of possibilities. Jane stood on tiptoe and pulled his mouth down to hers. Tasting him, she met his tongue thrusts with her own and drove her fingers through his thick hair.

"I'm trying my best to stop this madness, but you persist in making me see reason," she murmured, her lips trailing down the side of his neck. "You're everything I've ever wanted in a man, Nic."

He caught her at the back of the knees and lifted her feet off the platform. She wrapped her legs around his waist and kissed him again with complete abandon. She loved the way his mouth suckled hers, the smell of him, the towering maleness of him. In his big hands, she felt petite and totally female.

When he knelt down she loosened her hold around his shoulders and leaned backward until her spine made contact with the wooden platform. He inched up her sweater, exposing her lace-covered breasts. His mouth fastened on one and the tip of his tongue nudged the pink center until the material was damp and her nipple was as hard as a pebble.

She pushed his sweater up and caressed his wide chest. Muscles bunched and knotted beneath her hands. His eyes darkened a shade and his breathing quickened. She knew the signs.

"If I get splinters in my backside, I'll hold you personally responsible," she teased him.

"I could never forgive myself if that happened. Allow me to take that risk." With a lift and a turn, he changed places with her. "Reach into my jeans pocket and you'll find a necessary ingredient to good lovemaking."

"Oh?" She dipped two fingers into the pocket and brought out the foil square. "You take the Boy Scout motto to heart, don't you?"

He laughed, his hands spanning her waist. "Sure do. I'm always prepared."

Surveying their leafy loft, she grimaced with sudden shyness. "It seems weird doing this in the open."

"It's our own private paradise." He hooked a hand behind her neck and brought her head down for his kiss.

That kiss led to another and time spun out of control. Amid frenzied words, panting breath and a flurry of motion, clothes were discarded and passion soared. Jane lowered herself on him slowly, watching pleasure tighten his features and squeeze his eyes shut.

They reached their pinnacle of desire together, emitting hoarse cries of joy and clinging to each other as their emotions boiled over. An eagle sailed overhead and squirrels chattered. A nippy breeze spread goose bumps across Jane's exposed skin and she reached for her bra and sweater.

"It's getting too chilly for this kind of outdoor activity," she said, getting a smile from him. She combed his mussed hair with her fingers. "When you built this tree house, did you have this in mind?"

"No. I built it as an observatory, not as a bachelor's penthouse."

"Will you ever be able to see it as a mere observatory again?"

"No, I guess not." He sprang to his feet, agile and gloriously naked. "I don't think it's cold out here. Feels great to me."

"That's because you're Tarzan and you're used to the elements."

"Right," he agreed with a wicked grin, "and that's because I trot around in my loincloth even when there is six inches of snow on the ground." He pounded his impressively male chest. "Head colds are no match for a he-man like me."

Jane grabbed his jeans and underwear and threw them at him. "Get dressed, show-off."

He stepped into his white jockeys and hitched them up over his lean hips. "Ouch!"

"What's wrong?"

Angling a glance over his shoulder, he frowned. "I think I *did* pick up some splinters in my backside."

Jane smothered a giggle. "Don't worry, he-man. I'll remove them for you."

"You will? You'd do that for me?"

Jane nodded, mischief dancing within her. "Uh-huh. With my teeth."

Nicolas widened his eyes, then narrowed them swiftly. "Why, Lady Jane, I do believe you have the devil in you." A down-and-dirty grin lifted one corner of his mouth. "I like that in a woman."

NICOLAS HELD OPEN a gunny sack and Amanda dropped another pinecone into it.

"I wish I didn't have to go home," she announced.

"Why? You like it at home, don't you?"

"Yes . . . when Mommy's there. She and Jerome are working all the time now." Her chest rose and fell with a long, suffering sigh. "Mommy's famous, Jerome says, and she's got to sing for people."

"Do you like Jerome? Is he a good father?"

She brushed her hands together, dislodging dusty soil. "He's not my father. My father lives in heaven."

Nicolas glanced away from her, telling himself to watch his words, but a sweet aching built around his heart. He couldn't stand that his own daughter thought he was dead. "What if he didn't?"

"Didn't what?" Mandy sat on the ground on a carpet of fallen leaves.

Nicolas swallowed, his heart pounding like a drum, his conscience screaming at him to curb his tongue. "What if your father didn't live in heaven?" He pointed up. "That heaven. What if your father lived in a place he thought of as heaven on earth. Would you be glad or sad?"

"You mean, what if my daddy was alive?"

Nic held his breath and nodded.

Mandy kicked at a bunch of gold leaves. "I'd be glad. I always wanted to know what he looked like. Mommy says she didn't take any pictures of him." She frowned. "She has pictures of everybody else. I wish she'd taken some of him 'cause I bet he was as handsome as a prince."

Nic grinned. "What if he wasn't?" He sat beside her on the leaves. "What if he was gap-toothed, short and fat and bald? Would you still want to see him?"

She giggled. "Yes."

"You sure?"

"Yes," she insisted, still giggling. "I'd love him no matter what he looked like." Her giggles stopped and she became as earnest as a priest. "Just like *Beauty and the Beast*. She loved the Beast even though he was terrible to look at and had claws for hands. She loved his good heart."

Utterly charmed by her, Nicolas wished he could take her in his arms and sprinkle kisses over her face. He wanted to hold her, hug her and tell her he'd never loved anyone so completely, so unguardedly. But he was guarded, he reminded himself. Shields were up, placed there by people who had kept him from his daughter. Why should he continue this game when it might be best for him and his daughter if she knew the truth?

"You wouldn't be upset if your father suddenly showed up? Maybe he didn't know about you, but now that he does, he wants to spend lots of time with you."

She nodded and speared him with a look that made him wonder if he'd underestimated her intelligence, her insight. "Do you know my daddy? Have you met him?"

Nicolas nodded.

"Is he still alive?"

Nicolas nodded, almost against his will.

Amanda rose to her knees, her green eyes alight with excitement. "Did you tell him about me?"

"He knows about you, Mandy, but he didn't know he had a daughter until just a few weeks ago."

"But Mommy said—"

"Your mommy was wrong. He's not dead." Nicolas examined her expression carefully, looking for any hint of sadness or anger. "Are you upset, funny face?"

She shook her head quickly, sending her curls dancing. "Uh-uh! Where is he? Does he have any other kids?"

"No. You are his only child." Guilt slammed into him, taking his breath and his courage. He directed his gaze away from her, ashamed for giving in to his own selfish needs and not considering hers or his agreement with Jane to wait. But it was so damned hard!

"Nic..." Amanda placed a small hand on his shoulder, then gave his shoulder a shake to make him look at her.

"Yes, Mandy?" He felt tears burn the backs of his eyes. Her face was so endearing, so precious. He saw Selena in her; he saw himself in her; he saw a modern miracle in her. That he and Selena could make such a beautiful child nearly bowled him over.

"Nic, are you my daddy?"

Words failed him as the earth tilted, tipped sideways.

"It's okay if you are," she said, all solemn and mature and heart wrenching.

"Why would you ask that, Mandy?" His voice was tight, full of emotion. He had no doubt that his facial expression was much the same.

"I think I remember seeing some pictures of you in Mommy's photo album at home. You and Mommy were hugging and laughing. Mommy said you were just a friend, but . . . well, are you my daddy?''

In that instant, he knew he'd rather cut out his tongue than lie to her. There had been enough lies in this child's life.

JANE FINISHED MAKING Mandy's bed, her thoughts full of Nic and her burgeoning love for him.

Did he have a clue how she felt? Did he know that she was already in love with him? Men were sometimes blind to such overt emotions in a woman. Gathering up Mandy's scattered clothing, she folded them and placed them on top of the dresser. She wondered how she would tell Selena, *if* she should tell her.

"Of course, I have to," she whispered to herself, hoping that by hearing the words she would feel compelled to carry them out. However, a root canal sounded easier to bear than Selena's reaction to such news. If she called her a Benedict Arnold before, what would she call her now?

"Aunt Jane?"

She turned around. Mandy stood just inside the room with Nic right behind her. Jane gathered a deep breath, amazed that she'd been so lost in her thoughts that she hadn't heard them.

Nic wore a peculiar expression, but Mandy was all smiles.

"What's up?" Jane asked, addressing Mandy. Heavens, she looked like Nic! Those eyes and her hair . . . and something about her mouth. Its shape, perhaps?

"He told me."

"Told you—?" Jane's heart stopped cold and a chill careened through her body as her gaze snapped to Nicolas. He grimaced. "What have you told her? *What have you done?*"

"What she has every right to know, that's what I told her," he said.

"He's my daddy," Mandy said. "He hasn't been in *that* heaven—" she pointed upward, then down at the blue carpet "—but in *this* one. You found him for me, didn't you, Aunt Jane?"

Shaking with anger and with her mind in a turmoil, Jane used all her reserve strength to keep her voice level. She didn't want to alarm Mandy, but she didn't want to confirm Nic's announcement yet. She had to think. She had to plan. Oh, damn him, why had he opened his big mouth?

"Sweetie, I'll tell you about this in a few minutes. I have to talk to Nic first." She gestured toward the clothes she'd stacked on the dresser. "Tell you what, you pack and I'll be in to help in a little bit."

"Pack?" Nic asked.

"We're not leaving, are we?" Mandy asked.

"Of course, we're leaving. We only came for Thanksgiving and the holiday is over. We have to get back home."

"But I thought we weren't leaving until tomorrow."

"We are leaving today," she said firmly, then forced a smile to her trembling lips. "Just do it, okay, Mandy?"

"Are you mad? You look mad."

"Yes, I am." Jane tweaked Mandy's button nose. "But not at you."

"I want to stay here with my daddy."

Jane sighed heavily. "Amanda, please mind me. You know that we have to get back to Texas. I'll answer all your questions later. Right now, we must pack and I must talk to Nicolas—alone." She pushed him from the room and closed the bedroom door behind her. Motioning toward the living room, she went first, her feet almost flying, her nerves unraveling.

Her anger exploded over her like a thunderclap. Whirling to face him, it was all she could do not to scream obscenities, which was totally out of character for her. What was happening? Was *this* love?

"You told her. Promises mean nothing to you, do they?" she charged.

"I didn't exactly promise—"

"The hell you didn't," she interrupted. "Maybe you didn't say those exact words, but the implication was there. You have done everything I've asked you *not* to do. I guess that tells me something. I finally get it. You don't give a damn about anything or anybody but yourself." She paced like a mad woman, betrayal churning in her gut and making her feel sick to her stomach.

"That's not true. I didn't intend to tell her. She asked. Point-blank. I couldn't lie to her."

"Once again, you've ruined everything. Don't you even care about your daughter and her feelings?"

"Yes, that's why I told her I'm her father." He ran a hand through his hair and stared at the floor. "Jane, don't go ballistic on me. Why keep it a big secret? I think it's about time. We get along. We like each other.

It's time to start a relationship as father and daughter."

"But you can't blurt out these things. She's a child and this is a life-changing event for her. I wanted her to get to know you better and then I'd tell her—*after* I'd spoken to Selena first, of course."

His gaze bounced to hers. "Selena will never agree to letting me have Amanda."

"Have Amanda?" Jane repeated, stunned.

"If I had to wait for Selena's permission, I'd be senile before I'd get to see my daughter."

"Back up, back up," Jane said, spinning one hand as if rewinding a film. "What do you mean by 'have Amanda'? Selena is and will always be Mandy's custodial parent."

"I want to be part of Mandy's life, that's all. But Selena is not going to consent to that."

"You don't know what she will do. But this isn't about her. It's about you and your behavior."

"Relax, okay? Amanda is a lot more resilient than you give her credit for. She's fine with this."

"Oh, really?"

"Yes, really," he drawled, then flung himself on the couch. He stretched out, crossed his ankles and shielded his eyes with one arm.

Jane jutted out one hip and glared at him. "You've known this child for a couple of days, and I've known her all her life, but you are now an expert on her." She moved closer to him, her anger clouding her judgment and changing her tongue into a dangerous weapon. "You're right, Nicolas. Parenting is definitely *not* your forte."

He removed his arm slowly to damn her with his eyes. "I haven't hurt her. You don't hear her crying, do you? I know what I'm doing. Trust me."

"You can't drop a bombshell on a kid, then stand back while she sorts through the debris. Lucky for Mandy, she has me and her mother to protect her from people like you." She spun away, intent on packing her bag in record time, but Nic's hand clamped on her upper arm and he jerked her to a stop.

"I don't deserve that, Jane. I told you about my brother in confidence and you throw it in my face?"

She closed her eyes, hating herself for being guilty as charged. "I thought I could trust you."

"And I thought you were on my side."

She wrenched free of him. "I've told you. I'm on Mandy's side. Now I'm going to pack and then I'd appreciate it if you would lead us to my rental car."

"Your flight isn't until tomorrow."

"I'll exchange the tickets for ones today. We're leaving."

"This is the kind of attitude that grates on me, Jane. You and Selena deciding when I can see my daughter and when I can't. This has got to stop."

"Nicolas, listen to me, please." She gripped his forearm. "If you exercise some patience and let me handle this, you and Mandy will have plenty of time together. But you must let me talk with Selena. I've got a lot of explaining to do. Give me time to do it. Please."

"You still plan on stating my case, even though you seem to think I'm a lousy parent?"

She let go of him, deflated by the explosion of anger and misfired words. "Nic, I don't think you'd be a lousy parent or I wouldn't be trying to find a way to tell Selena about this Thanksgiving visit without causing a permanent rift between us." Her love for him broke through her darker feelings. "Just let me handle it, okay?"

"You're not going to tell Mandy that I'm not her father, are you?"

"No, I won't confuse the issue more by denying it now." She sighed with distress. "You know, Thunderheart, you're not making my life any easier."

"I love her already, Jane," he said, his voice reminding her of rough velvet. "She's my flesh and blood and I won't let anyone come between us again."

"No matter who you hurt?"

"I don't want to hurt anyone."

"But you will, if you aren't careful." She left the room and was glad that he didn't follow her.

Chapter Twelve

Selena flung open her suitcases on the bed and stepped to the door. "Christine, you can unpack my things now." Then she motioned for Jane to follow her through the open French doors and out onto the balcony. "Christine has placed a tray out here for us. Come and have a cup of apricot tea and some oatmeal crispies."

"You baked cookies? You shouldn't have," Jane teased.

"I didn't," Selena drawled lazily with a roll of her eyes. "You know I only returned home a couple of hours ago. I haven't even seen Mandy yet. Why'd you leave her at Mother's house when you knew I'd be home by now?"

"I wanted to talk to you first. Mom will bring Mandy home soon." Jane sat in one of the padded wrought-iron chairs. "I'll serve since Christine is busy unpacking your suitcases and you've probably forgotten how to pour, it's been so long."

"Ha, ha." Selena selected one of the crisp cookies from the china plate. "You're just jealous because I no longer have to keep house or cook. I can enjoy my time at home and with my family now."

"I'm not jealous," Jane argued. "I'm happy for you."

"What did you want to talk about?"

"About Thanksgiving."

Selena arched a brow. "Well, I had a good one. Didn't you? How was Mother's little get-together?"

"I didn't spend Thanksgiving with Mom."

Selena took a sip of tea and studied Jane over the rim of the cup. She slowly replaced it in the saucer and sighed. "Very well, Jane. Out with it. You've done something bad and you're about to confess. I know the drill."

"I don't want you to yell at me. I want to discuss this in a calm, adult manner." Jane chewed on her lower lip, dreading the fight that she knew would ensue. Selena had a diva's temper and she used it often. "You're going to hate me when I tell you this."

"That's doubtful." Selena regarded her suspiciously. "Let me guess…this has something to do with Mandy."

Jane nodded.

"You took Mandy somewhere besides Mother's for Thanksgiving."

Jane nodded.

"You didn't take her to Disneyland again, did you? You are spoiling that child rotten. Not Disneyland?" Selena tapped a finger against her full lips. "Six Flags Over Texas? No? Then I give up."

"The Smokies." Jane winced, waiting for her sister to make the connection between the place and the person.

"As in, mountains?" Selena tipped her head to one side in thoughtful repose, then her eyes widened and she sucked in a breath. "You took her to see *him?*"

Jane held her breath and bobbed her head. The explosion was imminent, she told herself, resisting the urge to squeeze her eyes shut and clamp her hands over her ears.

"Did you tell Mandy he was her father?"

Regarding Selena cautiously, Jane released her breath. "I didn't. He did."

Selena bit into another cookie, leaned back in the chair and crossed her legs. She looked at the lagoon-shaped pool, which had been drained and would be left empty until late spring. "Is Mandy upset? Is that why she's at Mother's?"

"No. She's full of questions, some of which I answered, some of which I told her she'd have to ask you. That's why she's at Mom's. I wanted to let you know that she knows and that I'm so sorry. I told him I didn't want him to tell her. He promised he wouldn't, but then he did. You know how men are. They're from Mars and we're from Ve—"

"What was Mandy's reaction? Besides shock, of course," Selena interrupted Jane's nervous babbling. She swung one leg lazily and seemed not to have a care in the world.

"Uh, she's glad, I think. Having a real dad is exciting. She wants to know everything about him." Jane swayed forward to get a better look at Selena's face.

"Are you all right? It's okay if you yell at me. I *expect* you to scream your head off."

Selena swung her gaze around to Jane, but there was no insane anger shining in her eyes or distorting her classic features. "How did they react to each other? Did they get along?"

"Yes, they liked each other right off the bat. Nicolas didn't tell Amanda he was her father until the last day we were there. They had already become buddies." Jane crossed her arms to ward off a shiver. Selena's reaction was downright spooky.

"He was gentle with her? He was kind?"

"Sure. I can't imagine Nicolas being anything but. Selena, he hasn't changed all *that* much, has he? I know you, and you wouldn't have married a complete jerk or a brute."

"No, he was neither of those things. He was self-centered, self-righteous and selfish."

"The operative word here being 'self,'" Jane noted dryly. "He was in his 'me' period, I guess."

Selena moaned. "Not that goofy theory of yours again." Her smile took the sting from her words. "In any case, I hope he's changed and that he appreciates his daughter. She's the only good thing that came out of our time together."

"What went so wrong with that relationship, Sis?"

Selena examined Jane from the corner of her eye as if debating with herself on whether to answer that question, then she capitulated. "Too young, too fast, too shallow."

"The operative word here being—"

"'Too,'" Selena jumped in. "Beat you." She tapped her cup with a long fingernail. "You're a poor hostess. My cup has been empty for five minutes."

"Oh, dear! Don't tell Miss Manners or I'll be drummed out of the corps." Jane laughed and gave Selena a refill. "You're in a great mood. I thought we'd be screaming at each other by now and I'd be crying and you'd be telling me that you'll never speak to me again."

"The day is young." Selena sent her a sinister smirk. "Actually, I've been yelling and screaming all through the holiday and I'm tired of it."

"That sounds horrible. You and Jerome didn't have a good time with your friends?"

"Our friends were charming, as usual, but Jerome was a complete mule. If I didn't adore him, I would order him out of my life." She flicked one hand in a patented diva gesture often used with the phrase, "Off with his head."

"Was he being a temperamental genius?"

Selena sobered suddenly and stared moodily at the empty pool. "He's happy to have *grown* children. He wants to devote his time to me and my career." A frown pleated the skin between her wide-set eyes. "He is determined that I place Amanda in that boarding school."

Jane groaned. "Not *that* again. Just tell him no, Selena. She's *your* daughter." Something her sister had said registered and Jane sat forward. "Hey, you mean, you *don't want* Mandy to go to that school?"

"Of course not."

"But you've been saying that it's a good school and a great place for a young lady—"

"I've been trying to talk myself into it because Jerome is insistent that Mandy be placed there. He says it will be too hard to travel with her. I said she could stay with Mother, but she's planning three trips herself next year."

"Yeah, where to?"

"Mexico, the Orient and Alaska," Selena said, ticking them off on her fingers. "Ever since she joined that senior citizens' travel club, all she does is plan trips and scout for low airfares and discounts on hotels." She blew at the tea before taking a sip. "And I can't leave her with you because it will interfere with your work, not to mention your life."

"I'd be glad to have her, but I don't get home until after eight some nights and sometimes I work all weekend, especially when my orders stack up around the style shows."

"I have to find a solution to this," Selena admitted. "I can't sweep it under the rug and I can't change Jerome's mind."

"Why do you have to? Like I said, she's your child."

"Yes, and Jerome is my husband, and what kind of life would it be for Amanda, being dragged around the country by a busy mother and a stepfather who isn't interested in fathering?"

"I see your point." Jane fell back in the chair, trying not to hate Jerome. She couldn't put the blame solely on him. He had never pretended to be interested in being a father figure to Mandy. He'd told Selena that he was madly in love, but he didn't want to marry her if she expected to have more children or if she needed a man to help her raise her child. Selena had married him, anyway, thinking Mandy would charm Jerome into changing his mind. It hadn't happened.

"It's my fault," Selena said bleakly. "But I won't make Mandy pay for my mistakes. I love Jerome with all my heart, but not at the expense of her happiness. I just don't think she'll like being in that boarding school. She loves having family around. She needs that security."

"I agree."

Selena shifted onto one hip, leaning closer to Jane. "So tell me, how did Nicolas react to Amanda? Did he seem natural with her or awkward? Did he know how to talk to her or was he condescending? I recall that he could be *very* condescending."

"He was wonderful with her, Selena. I was thinking I might have done the wrong thing, but then he saw Mandy and the look on his face—" She stopped, surprised to be swamped by her emotions at the memory. She had to swallow hard and blink away the sting of tears before she could continue. "It was instant love and there was never a moment of awkwardness. They bonded like Super Glue."

"That's interesting. Encouraging."

Jane clutched Selena's arm. "Are you thinking...you aren't really considering letting Mandy stay with Nic while you're on tour. Oh, Selena. *Are you?*"

"I'm rolling it over in my mind. Will you let go? You've cut off my circulation." She jiggled her arm free. "Good heavens, Jane, control yourself. I haven't made any decision. I'm only toying with the idea.

Frankly, I'm quite concerned about the kinds of influence Nicolas would have on my child. He isn't a sterling role model, after all.''

"Oh, but he is,'' Jane argued. "He's a wonderful man.''

Selena looked askance at her. "Down, girl. I didn't say he was a two-headed monster. He certainly has won you over to his corner, hasn't he?''

"I want what's best for Mandy,'' Jane said, feeling like a wolf in sheep's clothing.

"That makes two of us, but I don't know if Nic is best. He told me he never wanted children—''

"Then,'' Jane amended. "He said he didn't want children then. Your marriage was rocky and his business was sinking like the *Titanic*, so the timing was lousy, you have to admit.''

"I take it that you two have discussed this at great length.''

"No, I asked and he answered. Selena, people have a right to change their minds. Actually, I think it would be better for this world if more people thought long and hard about having kids *before* they had them.''

"Oh, so I was wrong to get pregnant?''

"No, but you didn't conceive at a joyous, stable moment in your marriage.''

"True. Those moments were woefully rare. But it's different this time. I want this marriage to work because Jerome is everything I've ever wanted in a husband. He adores me, he lets me have my way most of the time, he thinks I'm the greatest singer in the world and he doesn't want me to cook or clean or wait on him. He's perfect.''

"Perfect for you, but what about Mandy?"

"Yes, that's the fly in the ointment, and that's why I had a horrible Thanksgiving. I cried, I pleaded, I pouted, but he wouldn't budge."

"Mom doesn't think you should place Mandy in that boarding school, either. I asked Mandy, and she said she'll run away if you send her there."

"I'm not sending her."

"You're not?"

Selena glanced upward. "No. Did you ever really think I would?" She made a scoffing noise. "So tell me more about his life-style these days. Who is he boffing?"

"Wh-what?" Jane choked and felt as if her face had become a furnace.

"Oh, please," Selena cut in, "don't tell me he doesn't have a lady friend. Nicolas was always ready for a sexual romp. That's another nice thing about Jerome—he has slowed down and doesn't expect it every night. Once a week suits him, and it suits me. Mostly on Wednesdays, but if we skip a week, it's no big deal."

Jane bit down on her lip to keep from giggling. *Once a week on Wednesdays?* Nope, she couldn't imagine Nicolas Thunderheart being satisfied with such a skimpy routine.

"He's got someone," Selena said, a smugness apparent in her tone. "He didn't tell you? Did he pretend to be all alone in his wilderness? A Tarzan without his Ja—" She stopped abruptly, her eyes narrowing.

"What?" Jane asked, feeling like a parrot...right, in the sightings of a powerful rifle. "Why are you looking at me like that?"

"A thought just struck me. An awful, sickening thought."

"Maybe you should keep it to yourself," Jane suggested brightly. "Want some more tea?"

"No, what I want is for you to look me straight in the eye and tell me that you haven't fallen in—"

A door slammed somewhere inside the house and then feet pounded on the stairs.

"Mom? Mommy? Where are you?" Amanda called.

"In here, darling." Selena rose from the chair and went inside the bedroom. "Hello, there, stranger. Did you miss me?"

"Yes, yes, yes! Did you bring me anything?"

"You gold digger! Yes, I brought you a hug and a kiss."

Smiling, and relieved by her niece's timing, Jane joined Selena and Amanda in the bedroom. "Hi, again, Mandy. Where's your grandmother?"

"She didn't stay. She just let me off. I think she had a meeting with a travel agent."

"Sounds like Mother," Selena said, holding Mandy at arm's length and looking her over as if she expected to see a difference in the child. "Your Aunt Jane says you learned the truth about Nicolas."

"Yes. How come you never told me about him being my daddy?"

"Maybe I didn't want to share you." Selena shrugged. "I lost track of him, that's all. He never tried to find you, either."

"Selena, that's not true," Jane said. "Tell her the truth or nothing at all, but no more lies."

"Lies?" Selena bristled. "He's a paragon of truth and I'm a liar? Is that what you're saying?"

"You know he didn't contact Amanda because he never knew about her," Jane insisted, refusing to be thrown off the track. "It's not fair to Mandy to make her think he didn't want her in his life."

"As you can see, Amanda, your aunt and I are still thrashing this out. It's boring, so you are excused. I brought you a new video game and it's in the game room."

"Thanks." Mandy kissed her mother's cheek. "Mommy, I really am glad he's my daddy. I think he's handsome and brave and funny."

Selena's face tightened and her smile was forced. "I'm glad, dear heart. Now go play and we'll be downstairs in a little bit."

"Okay, but no more fighting," Mandy said, shaking a finger and giving them a stern look before grinning broadly and scampering out of the room.

"She's a sweet imp," Jane said, crossing her arms and hugging herself as family pride swelled within her. For an instant, she imagined herself as a mother, and for the first time, she didn't shy away from the notion. A wife and a mother, she mused, and another image flooded her mind, one of her and Nicolas.

"Forget my daughter for a moment, and let's talk about you," Selena said, studying Jane as if she were a witness who'd just been sworn in. "Once upon a time, you had a crush on Nicolas. You admit that, don't you?"

An uneasiness wormed through Jane. "Yes, once upon a time," she answered cautiously, aware that she was being fitted for a noose. "But it was an infatuation thing—I was young and I didn't even know him. Like when you went gaga for that rock star, remember? You saw him in concert three times in two weeks and you bought every magazine and—"

"Yes, yes, but we're not talking about me," Selena cut in. "Besides, that musician has never been part of our family and I doubt he ever will. It's also doubtful any of us will ever even meet him."

"Right, and I just admired Nicolas from afar." Jane spun around and went back onto the balcony. The air was getting too close in the bedroom. She breathed deeply and grabbed a cookie off the tray.

"Now that you've spent time with him," Selena said from behind her, "what do you think?"

"He's a nice man and he gets along well with Mandy." Jane crammed the rest of the cookie into her mouth and chewed frantically. When she was nervous, she ate, and she was suddenly ravenous.

Selena moved to stand beside her. "Jane, are you and Nicolas doing the hoochie-koochie?"

Jane tried to laugh, but her mouth was full of cookie and her heart wasn't in it.

"Before you laugh this off, remember that you and I are on a truth-telling mission here," Selena warned. "I'll be honest, if you will."

Jane swallowed the sugary food and brushed crumbs from the front of her blouse. "You mean you'll stop twisting facts to suit you? You'll quit telling Mandy that Nic never wanted to see her?"

"Yes," Selena agreed. "Okay, give. Answer me."

Jane closed her eyes for a moment to gather her courage. She felt the noose tighten around her neck. "I'm the one he's boffing now."

"I knew it," Selena announced, slapping her palms against the balcony railing. "I told Mother that Nic would do whatever he had to do to get Mandy away from me."

"What?" Jane glared at her. "What has sleeping with me got to do with that?"

"He's using you."

"He is not." She wished she could be as certain as she sounded. "And he didn't *have* to sleep with me. It wasn't a chore for him, and I didn't even have to beg. You know, Selena, you're coming mighty close to hurting my feelings."

"I don't mean to, Jane. But the man is ruthless, I tell you, and he'll do anything to get what he wants, and what he wants right now is my daughter."

"She's his daughter, too," Jane noted, not liking her sister at the moment. "This will probably come as a big shock to you, Sis, but Nic and I happen to care very much for each other. Do you think I'd go to bed with him if I weren't halfway in love with him already?"

Selena fell back a step in utter shock. "Bite your tongue, Jane. You can't be in love with him—even halfway."

A calm settled over her and the confusion she'd been wrestling with disappeared, leaving her with one shining certainty. "I *am* in love with him, Selena, and I hope and pray he loves me, too."

Selena leaned forward, one hand spread above her breasts. "But I was *married* to him. You *can't* be in love with him. It's too... too much like a soap opera plot."

"It's not so horrible. You don't have any feelings for him anymore, right?"

"Right. Doubly right!"

"Then there shouldn't be any awkwardness. You two were married briefly years ago. He's a different person now and so are you. Look at it this way, Mom won't have to break in a new son-in-law."

"Wait." Selena rested a hand on Jane's shoulder. "You aren't already thinking about marriage, are you? One roll in the hay... or wherever... and you're ready to commit yourself to him forever? That's what happened to me, Jane. I want you to be smarter than I was."

"Marriage hasn't been discussed, but I've never felt like this about any other man."

"You should be more concerned about what he's feeling for you and why."

"Selena, don't start, please. I'm not going to run off and marry him in a blaze of lust."

"Like I did," Selena tacked on.

"Exactly. I'm more concerned about his relationship with Mandy than with his one with me."

"I don't want any threats from him and I don't want any more secret visits between him and Mandy."

Jane nodded. "Done. You have my promise. I've told him you are calling the shots from here on in."

"Good. I have a lot to think about."

"Honestly, Selena, he doesn't want to cause any trouble. He just wants to have a part in her life."

"Not take over her life and ruin mine?"

"No. Not that. Never that," Jane assured her. "He's not a black-hearted villain."

"I know." Selena turned aside and looked across trees and rooftops of the posh Dallas suburb. "But if he tries anything funny I'll unleash an army of lawyers on him and make him wish he'd never met me or Mandy or you."

Jane shivered at the tone of Selena's voice. She was dead serious. Nic didn't want Selena as his enemy in this. Jane only hoped he knew that.

Chapter Thirteen

The red T-bird cornered neatly and answered Jane's request for acceleration with a deep purr and a blur of scenery. She wrapped the fingers of one hand loosely around the padded steering wheel and popped in a cassette tape with the other. The hip, brandy-smooth voice of Natalie Cole poured from the sound system. Jane smiled. Life was good.

Life would be perfect if Nicolas Thunderheart had a telephone.

Eight days had passed since Selena's return and their consequent heart-to-heart. Jane had wanted to contact Nic and tell him how well the discussion had gone and how pleased she was that Selena was actually considering stepping aside and allowing Nic and Mandy to spend time together. But he had no phone, and Jane didn't want to put her thoughts in an abbreviated fax that would be spit out in the drugstore to await a visit from Nicolas.

Jerome was already planning the next business trip for Selena, which would send them to New York right after Christmas for a production of *La Traviata*. They'd be there until the end of January. And what of

Mandy? Jane knew that this question plagued Selena. While Jerome kept dropping hints about the boarding school right after the Christmas holidays, Selena was stoically silent. Jane suspected her sister was getting used to the idea of her daughter living with Nicolas Thunderheart.

Yesterday when Jane had talked to Mandy on the phone, she had said that her mother had been asking about Nic and his house and if Mandy thought she might like spending time in the Smoky Mountain wilds. This morning Selena had called and asked Jane to join her and Mandy for brunch on the patio. The day was warm for December with a light breeze stirring the fallen leaves. Jane suspected that Selena had come to a decision.

High spirits bubbled inside her as she stopped the car in the circular driveway beside Selena's palatial home. She turned off the engine and listened to the chirping of birds and the breeze singing in the trees. Immediately, her thoughts took wing and flew to that house on the bridge and the man who resided in it.

"I miss you," she whispered to the blue sky above, seeing only his green eyes and devilish grin, feeling only the rough velvet of his touch, the gentle insistence of his kisses. "Do you miss me?"

Gently tapping the steering wheel with her fist, she vented a bit of her frustration. Something would have to be done, she thought. Either he trekked into town and called her every day or two, or... they ended this long-distance romance and moved in together. That she'd even think about packing up and moving to the Smokies startled her and made her even more aware of how much Nic had come to mean to her. She was restless without him, aimless, lonely. If he didn't feel the same way, she'd never forgive him!

Laughing at herself, Jane emerged from the car and walked with a definite spring to her step around to the back of the house where brunch would be served. As she expected, Selena was waiting for her, but Mandy was nowhere in sight.

"Did the kid take a powder on us again?" Jane asked, approaching her sister, who sat in one of the patio chairs arranged around a glass-topped table. "You ever get the feeling she thinks we're as dull as dishwater?"

"There is nothing dull about this day, I can assure you," Selena said, shifting her gaze slowly, accusingly, to Jane. "Have you, by chance, heard from your boyfriend lately?"

A tingling apprehension inched up her spine. "No, but I was just wishing I could get in touch with him. Why?"

"I've heard from him."

"You have?" Jane's heart soared, but something in Selena's attitude gave her pause. "There's nothing wrong with him, is there? He's okay?"

Selena nodded at the empty chairs. "Have a seat."

"Selena, tell me."

"Sit down," she said, her dead calm scaring Jane into obeying. "He sent me this today—by a process server." She handed over three or four pages folded in thirds.

Jane flattened the pages on the table and ran her eyes over the legal phrases, cutting through to the heart of the message. Her spirits plummeted and the day that had been so sunny and bright was suddenly doom and gloom.

Nicolas Thunderheart had petitioned for custody of his only child, Amanda Jane, and the preliminary hearing was scheduled six days before Christmas.

JANE DIDN'T NEED directions or a guide this time to find Nic's house. She went there with uncanny accuracy, stomping through the woods, her purpose solid in her mind like a stone. She wasn't mad anymore, not like she had been two days ago when Selena had shown her the legal petition Nic had filed. No, she was past the anger. Now she wrestled with a deep, abiding hurt in her heart. Once again, he had proven that he trusted no one, not even her.

Seeing the house again gave her no joy. She barely glanced at it as she entered the clearing and searched for signs of life. Laundry fluttered on a line—jeans and sweatshirts, socks and underwear. Jane strolled toward the stream, expecting to find Nicolas fishing or doing more laundry there. Downstream, a man swam for shore. Water sluiced down his nude body as he emerged from the stream and climbed the grassy bank. Sunlight glinted off his dark hair. From a distance, he looked as if he'd lost weight. He reached for a towel folded neatly on a rock.

Jane cupped her hands around her mouth, fashioning a megaphone. "Hey, there, Tonto! I'm back and I'm on the warpath."

He jerked in surprise, then made a wild grab for the towel. Jane smiled, ruefully, bitterly.

"I've seen the merchandise, so relax," she called out to him.

"Jane?"

Spinning around, she stared, aghast, at Nicolas, fully clothed and wearing a bemused expression. Her heart crammed itself into her throat before she looked back at the other man—the nude one way downstream. He scrambled to tuck the towel securely at his waist and conceal his family jewels.

"Oh, my God!" Jane placed a hand to her gaping mouth. "Who...I thought he was you."

"He's my brother."

"Richie?"

Nic nodded, grinning, then gestured to the other man. "Get dressed and I'll introduce you," he told him.

"Right," Rich called back, then jogged to the house, the ends of the towel flapping in the breeze.

Jane covered her face with her hands and felt her cheeks heat up like a furnace. "I can't meet him now. I've seen his—*everything*."

Nicolas laughed. "So you've seen his best parts. What's so bad about that?"

Recovering from the shock and embarrassment, Jane removed her hands from her face and put herself back on track. She gave him a sweeping glance, taking in his scuffed boots, faded jeans and ragged sweatshirt stained with perspiration. He carried an ax, and she realized he'd been chopping firewood. She wanted to ask him why he'd knifed her in the back, but she knew that would sound whiny and she wanted to be strong and unrelenting in her damnation of his actions.

"You don't seem surprised to see me."

"I thought you might bring Selena with you."

"No. She isn't interested in talking with you—now. You've ruined everything, you know."

Nic juggled the ax. "You didn't, by chance, bring my daughter. I'd love for her to meet her uncle."

"I only brought myself. You'll be lucky to ever see your daughter again."

"I hope you haven't come here just to hurl threats at me, Jane. I thought about my options before I filed the petition. I decided it was best to let the courts intervene. I know you have boundless faith in your sister's judgment, but I don't. The more I thought about it, the more convinced I was that Selena wouldn't turn over a new leaf. She kept Amanda a secret, so she'll obviously do what she must to continue to keep me away from my daughter."

"Why did you make me think that we were in agreement?"

"I didn't mean to do that. I did agree with you at first, but then I started thinking... remembering how Selena can be a first-class bi—"

"People change, Nicolas. Isn't that what you've been telling me? How you've changed?"

He gathered in a deep breath. "I did what I thought was right. I'm a man of action, Jane. I can't just sit back and wait for Selena to make decisions for me."

She slid the straps of her backpack off her shoulders. "I had her in your corner, Nic. You blew it." She shook her head, the past dreadful days and nights catching up to her. "Can I stay overnight?"

"Sure. Why don't you stay forever?"

She winced as the question she'd been hoping he would ask sliced through her. "It's too late for that." She started to turn away, but he caught her by the arm.

"Jane, don't do this. My battle with Selena doesn't have to come between us."

She gaped at him. "It already has, Nic, and you're a fool if you ever thought any different. I started this avalanche and I have to see this disaster through to the end. It's already destroyed what might have been for us. I just pray it doesn't destroy my niece next."

"You didn't start this. Selena did."

"And this didn't have to be a battle. You're the one who turned it into one with your stupid court petition."

Pulling free of his hold, she marched away from him and stormed into the house and up to the main level. Encountering Richie in the living area, she found it difficult to look him in the face.

"I'm decent now," he said, his voice not as deep as Nic's but having the same inflections and Southern accent. He extended one hand. "Hi. I'm Richard Thunderheart. You're Jane Litton, right?"

"Right." She shook his hand. "Nice to meet you. Nicolas is quite proud of you. Aren't you in the navy?"

"Yes. I'm on leave."

"So how long are you staying here?"

"Only until the end of the week. I'm going to spend the holidays with my girl." He smiled shyly. "We just got engaged and I'm going to meet her folks in New Jersey."

"Congratulations. Have you set a date?"

"Valentine's Day." He blushed.

Charmed, Jane reached out and squeezed his upper arm, finding it hard with muscle. He was tall, maybe an inch or two shorter than Nic. "Valentine's Day. How romantic."

"Maybe you and Amanda can come to the wedding. I was thinking that she could be our flower girl."

Jane felt her smile slip. What had Nicolas told his brother? Had he painted a pretty picture of domestic happiness for his brother? She hoisted her heavy backpack.

"Wonder where I can stow my stuff. You're in the guest room, I gather."

"Yeah, but I can sleep on the couch tonight and you can sleep in there."

"No. Don't be silly. I'll crash on the couch, but I'll put my things in the guest room if you don't mind."

"Let me." He took the backpack from her. "You sure you don't want to sleep in the guest room?"

"I'm sure. I'm only staying one night and the couch is comfy." She followed him to the bedroom where he placed her backpack on the spare twin, the one Mandy had slept in before. "Nic says he's going to give this room to Mandy and build an additional guest room downstairs."

"That's nice, although a bit premature." She unzipped her backpack and removed the extra pair of jeans, knit shirt and turtleneck sweater. "I don't know what Nicolas told you, but it's not a sure thing that Mandy will ever stay here."

"Nic is confident she will."

"Bully for Nic." She sighed, knowing she shouldn't be snippy with Richie, but finding it hard to curb her tongue. "I guess you were surprised to discover you had a niece."

"Surprised and happy for Nic." He sat on the other bed and motioned for Jane to sit opposite him on the other. "This is a second chance for Nic, and he needed one. He's been carrying around a lot of guilt and this might be a way for him to get rid of it."

"He told me about how he wasn't there for you when you were a kid," she admitted. "I think he's being too hard on himself. What do you think?"

"Yeah, I suppose he is." Richie leaned back against the wall and locked his hands behind his head. "I hated him back then. I hated him for ignoring me, then tracking me down after I ran away like he gave a rat's behind what happened to me."

"He did care what happened to you."

"Oh, yeah? Were you around then to witness this?"

Justly chastised, Jane could do nothing but shrug off his well-aimed observation.

"He was wrapped up in his own life and with your sister, too. She didn't want me around, either."

Jane scowled. "She never told me that."

"I overheard her talking to Nic. She asked him what he was going to do with me and that she didn't want to start out married life with a teenage hoodlum living with them."

Jane sucked in a breath. "She's never said a bad thing about you in my presence."

He bobbed one shoulder. "It's history, but it left scars, you know? If I hadn't had my uncle to raise me, I'd be in prison or dead probably."

"You know that Nicolas loves you, don't you?"

"Sure. I know it now."

"He *says* he's a different person now." She tried to hide her irritation with Nicolas, but she knew she was doing a poor job of it.

"Yeah, he is." Richie grinned, his green eyes crinkling at the corners. His hair was cut short. Dark brown, like Nic's, it showed a tendency to curl. "So am I. Hell, I'm nothing like I was back then. Losing my parents sent me into a tailspin. I hated Nic for not crumbling under the loss, like I did. He went right along with his life like nothing had happened. I never saw him cry or grieve. He made the arrangements, went to the services, paid for everything, then went back to work. That was it. Our parents were dead, but that barely made a ripple in his life."

"He was driven back then. Too driven. I think, too, that he was unhappy. That's probably why he jumped into a marriage with my sister. They barely knew each other when they ran off and got married in a frenzied, slightly inebriated rush of lust."

Richie chuckled. "Yeah, I remember Uncle Vern calling him a damn fool for getting married instead of waiting to sober up first." He stretched his arms above his head. "I lived with him and Selena for about five months. It was a real zoo. For the first two months they were crazy for each other, but then they started fighting and the honeymoon was definitely over. I guess Nic's business was going under about that time and Selena was sick of hearing about it and having to squeeze every penny."

"Selena never was one to save grocery coupons."

"Right before I cut out, I heard her yell at him, 'We don't love each other, we just wish we did.'" He nodded, sagely. "That about summed up their feelings for each other."

"I bet you felt as if you were caught in a vise."

He smiled sadly. "Exactly." He smoothed his hands along his jeaned thighs. "But, hey, we all have lessons to learn and burdens to carry. Uncle Vern gave me what I needed and Nic finally opened his eyes and saw that he was clinging to some pretty shallow stuff." He glanced around. "He's got his act together now. He'll be a good father to his little girl."

Jane chose to examine a hangnail instead of his intent expression. "I get the feeling you don't usually share so much with a stranger. You're not stating your brother's case for him, are you? You weren't coached by big brother, by any chance."

"No way. But I did want to talk to you. I wanted you to know Nic has learned valuable lessons. He wants to be a father to Amanda. He *really* wants that."

"They got along fine over Thanksgiving."

"There you go. It's a beginning, right?"

She smiled at him. "Right. But only that."

He nodded, then eyed her with open curiosity. "So you and my brother are an item, huh? It must be mind warping falling in love with your ex-brother-in-law."

Jane shifted uncomfortably. "Warp is a good word for it. Who said I was falling in love? Nic?"

"I deduced that on my own."

"We're not an item anymore." She ran a hand down her face, fighting off a spate of self-pity. "I was walking a tightrope and he pushed me off."

"Yeah? Well, he's been pushed off a few times, too. Your sister gave him the heave-ho when he needed someone to give him a steady hand for balance. Prescott tripped him up and sent him tumbling again. Can you blame the guy for not trusting people?"

"That doesn't mean he has to trample them."

"He's learned not to believe that anyone else will come through for him. Even love can't heal every wound. I speak from experience. I love the guy with all my heart, but that little guy I was once is still inside me somewhere, and he hasn't totally forgiven his big brother. The grown-up understands that Nic was treading water to keep afloat back then and didn't have the time or know-how to be father of the year. But the kid will always be mad as hell at Nic for not being there for him."

"I'm mad as hell at him," she admitted. "And hurt. Deeply hurt. I thought he trusted me."

"He trusts no one."

"Not even you?"

A sad smile tilted up the corners of his mouth. "Nope, although he'd deny that." Richie leaned forward suddenly and grasped her hands. "I think you'll be good for him, Jane. If anyone can rebuild his bridge of trust in his fellow human being, it's you. When he talks about you, he does so with such warmth. I've never seen him so openly taken with anyone before—other than Amanda, of course."

Soft footsteps sounded in the hallway and Richie released her hands and stood before Nicolas rounded the corner and looked into the room.

"I'm glad to see that you two are getting to know each other," he drawled, "but I was wondering if anyone is hungry."

"I am," Rich said.

"Good, then you can set the table while I heat up the potato soup and slice the bread."

"Aye-aye, sir." He essayed a snappy salute in true navy fashion, then marched from the room.

"What do you think of him?" Nic asked.

"I think, of the two brothers, he's got his head on straight and his heart in the right place." She stood and placed a hand on Nic's chest, giving him a slight push. "If you'll excuse me, I'd like to change before dinner."

"I can't watch?"

His teasing didn't chide her into a good mood, but only sparked her ire. It hurt that he thought she could even jest under the circumstances. "You don't get it, do you? We're not taking up where we left off. I don't sleep with men I don't trust, and I don't trust you anymore."

Retreating from the room, he placed a hand against the door to prevent her from shutting it in his face. "Why are you here if you dislike me so much?"

"To ask you to withdraw that petition."

He shook his head. "You're wasting your time."

"It's mine to waste." She shoved at the door. "We'll talk after dinner."

He removed his hand from it. "Jane, I know you're mad at me, but this isn't the end of the world."

"No, but it very well could be the end of us." She shut the door, but not before she saw his grimace of regret. That chink in his armor gave her hope.

NICOLAS FED ANOTHER STICK or two of fatwood to the dying fire and added another hefty log. The fire caught and flamed, throwing a glowing light across Jane's face. Her eyelashes cast long shadows down her cheeks. She sat ramrod straight on the couch as if she were made of tempered steel.

"It's getting downright cold at night now. You'll be warmer in my bed."

"The couch is fine," she said stiffly, and Nic suddenly needed her smile, craved the sound of her laughter.

"But you'll be much warmer in my—"

"Cut the teasing chatter. I'm not in the mood. I wish I could make light of this, but I can't. I see no humor in the situation you've placed us in."

He crossed his arms against his chest, wishing he could hold her and dam her hurtful words with his mouth. "Well, we're alone now, so let's have this out and be done with it."

She released a barking laugh. "Like it can be handled that easily."

"It can, if you'll see reason."

"Me? Ha! How can you not see that your actions have torn our relationship and forced me to join forces against you?" She shot up from the couch, her hands balled into tight fists. "Do you actually prefer a court battle? Do you want to put your child through that ugliness?"

"I appreciate you being straight with me and telling me about Mandy, Jane, but I can handle it from here on in. A judge will hear both sides and deliver an unprejudiced decision as to who should have custody of Mandy. If Selena doesn't have time to raise her, then the judge will determine that Mandy should live with me."

"Why do we need an outsider making these decisions? What makes you think that Selena wouldn't have agreed to this without a judge forcing it on her?"

"Selena kept Mandy from me all these years, so why would she suddenly hand her over to me?"

"Because I was talking her into it." She paced in front of the couch. "She's not mindless, you know. Selena wants what is best for Mandy and she was beginning to see that you were offering the perfect solution. But that petition ruined it. She now firmly believes you haven't changed, that all you're interested in is exacting your pound of flesh."

He blinked in amazement. "What's that mean?"

"She thinks you're trying to hurt her for throwing in the towel when you needed her the most. Selena says you're being selfish and not thinking about how Mandy will be damaged by this. She says you're only interested in paying her back for deserting you when you were crashing and burning in the business world."

He laughed, bitterness churning in his stomach. "Sounds like Selena. Everything is about her."

"Funny, she said the same thing about you. Personally, I think you're both being selfish and not giving a thought to your daughter's feelings."

He grabbed her arm, making her stand still. "You're wearing a hole in the floor."

He couldn't help caressing her arm through the cream, knit shirt. Her hair was golden in the firelight and her skin was flawless. He stroked her soft cheek and rubbed the pad of his thumb across her lower lip. He refused to believe that his actions had ended his relationship with Jane. Not when he was touching her and staring into her beautiful eyes. He'd make her understand that Selena couldn't be trusted. No one could when it came to getting what you wanted, what was most important in your life. He'd learned that the hard way.

"Once this custody thing is settled, we can put it behind us and concentrate on us," he told her. "You'll see."

"Do you actually think I could take up with you again after you've forced my sister to surrender her child to you? And what if Selena wins this custody battle? Will you welcome me back here? I doubt it."

"What we have doesn't hinge on Mandy, Jane."

"Oh, doesn't it? I wonder."

He didn't like the suspicion lurking in her eyes. Dropping his hands from her, he stepped back. "The bottom line is I couldn't trust Selena to do the right thing."

"And what about me? You couldn't trust me, either?"

"Jane, be reasonable. We've only known each other a short time. I couldn't be certain you wouldn't finally side with Selena, no matter what she decided to do."

"Why does there have to be sides to this? Why couldn't you give *me* the benefit of the doubt and let me reason with Selena? She was coming around. It would be much better if this was her decision and you two could mend your bridges and raise your daughter without hostilities."

"Yes, in a perfect world that would work."

A log in the fireplace snapped in two and sent out sparks and glowing embers. Nicolas stepped away from the flames and bumped into Jane. His arms came around her instinctively. Her hands moved against his chest, then up to his shoulders.

"Jane, I haven't spent a night since we met without wanting you beside me," he said, the words falling from him in a rush of longing. Her slender body pressed against him. With a groan, he crushed her mouth beneath his and explored the sweet depths of her with his tongue. Winning her back suddenly became all-important. "Come to my room, Jane," he whispered against her warm, moist lips.

"No, Nic."

Her eyes held a profound sadness that tore at his heart and made him realize the damage he'd done. He hadn't thought—he'd only been concerned about getting his daughter and hadn't considered all the ramifications... until now.

"We could make love until dawn and that wouldn't change anything. You still wouldn't trust me, and I can't settle for anything less." She turned her face away from his.

Nic let go of her, her cold determination defeating him. Fear tightened his chest and throat. Fear? Yes, he admitted to himself. Suddenly, he was afraid he might lose her if he couldn't make her understand. "Jane, it's not that I don't trust you. I don't trust Selena."

She released a long, weary-laden sigh. "Nicolas, I want you to reconsider this custody battle. There is still time to drop it. I hope you'll see you're not only squaring off against Selena, but against her family, which includes me."

"Don't you think I've already considered that?" he asked, exasperated. "Jane...I..." He swallowed, surprised that the words were hard to say when he felt them so strongly in his heart. "I th-think I'm falling in love with you."

"You *think?*" She shook her head and her soft laugh was unpleasant sounding, not what he'd been wishing for. "Well, now, that *is* funny, and the joke's on me."

"Jane..." He reached for her, remorse writhing in him, but she darted away.

"I want to go to bed," she said, her voice strained. She stared at the couch, refusing to look at him. "Good night."

"Jane, I'll think about what you've said." He ran a hand around the back of his neck while his mind whirled, trying to find a way to ease her pain and his, to make her understand that love was uncommon in his life and that trust was something one earned over the long haul.

She sat on the couch and stared out the window. The panes reflected her image and Nic saw tears brimming in her eyes.

"I hope you will think about what I've said, Nicolas, and take it to heart."

"I will." His head ached and he suddenly felt as if he were carrying an elephant on his shoulders. "I know one thing. I don't want to lose Mandy—or you." He saw tears glisten on her cheeks. "Jane?"

She turned away from him, making it clear she didn't want anything from him, not even his company. "Good night, Nic."

Staring at her, his gut tied itself in knots and his heart constricted painfully. He felt his convictions waver as doubt clouded his mind. He'd been so sure before, so certain he'd taken the right course of action. But that was before her tears, before he'd seen her disappointment in him.

Forcing one foot in front of the other, he went to his bedroom to wage war with himself. Was it his destiny to disappoint everyone who meant anything to him? he wondered, unable to shut out the memory of Jane's tears.

Was Mandy the next in line?

Chapter Fourteen

Sitting in the back of the chauffeured limo with Selena, Jane dreaded the confrontation ahead and it was only the first step in what would probably develop into a legal brawl. She assumed Nicolas would show up at the preliminary hearing instead of just sending his attorney this time. It would be their first face-to-face meeting since she'd left his home. Her visit had resolved nothing, other than a deeper understanding of Nicolas Thunderheart.

Her talk with Richie had illuminated some of Nic's darker qualities. When he had said that Nicolas trusted no one, Jane had recognized her own fatal mistake in assuming that because Nic cared for her, he trusted her to do the right thing. Barrett Prescott had fatally wounded Nic's trust in his fellow man and Selena had probably finished it off. Realizing this, Jane had known that her visit, her pleas, her rationalizing, were pointless. The bottom line was trust and Nic wasn't willing to give it.

The limo telephone buzzed and Selena answered it. Listening to her part of the conversation, Jane surmised that it was Jerome calling. The exchange was brief.

"That was my darling husband," Selena said, replacing the receiver. "He's worried about me." She glanced at Jane. "But I think you're in worse shape than I am. Are you feeling all right?"

Jane massaged her right temple. "Not really. I hate this, Selena. I hate this mess and it's all my fault."

"Oh, stop it. We've gone over and over this. I've forgiven you for poking your nose in my business, so you should forgive yourself now. How could you have known that Nicolas is a back-stabbing fathead?"

Jane smiled briefly. "I wish I could hate him, but I can't. I keep thinking how I would feel in his shoes and I know I'd be bitter and striking out at those who kept my child from me."

"You're taking his side?" Selena asked, turning on the seat to glare at her.

Jane gritted her teeth. "I'm *not* taking sides on this, Selena. I told you that. I only want what is best for Mandy."

"Is that so?" Selena flicked a thread from her fitted black skirt. "Well, a court battle between her parents isn't going to be a picnic, you know. She's not here to witness it, but she'll feel it. Children are very sensitive."

"Speaking of which, do you remember much about the time when Richie stayed with you and Nic?"

Selena looked away quickly. "Not much. I remember not liking it."

"Why not?"

"Because we were newlyweds. And Richie wasn't all that pleasant to be around. He was a little punk."

"Was he violent?"

"No, he was...insolent. He and Nic had shouting matches. Nic would ground him and then expect me to keep the little monster in the house." She laughed bitterly. "Like I could make Richie do anything. The day he ran away was the first peaceful one I'd had since moving in with Nic."

"Did he sneak off?"

"No." Selena stared out the dark windows of the limo.

Jane regarded her shielded expression and sensed that she was struggling with something, and that whatever it was made her feel guilty. "If he didn't sneak off..." She let the rest fade away, hoping Selena would jump in.

"He..." Selena glanced sharply at Jane. "It's ancient history. I can't recall the nitty-gritty details."

"Okay, in broad strokes, tell me about when Richie ran away. When did you notice he was missing?"

Selena shut her eyes and seemed to quell a shiver. "He told me he was leaving."

Jane mulled this over for a few moments. "You're saying you *knew* he was leaving and you didn't try to stop him? Didn't you even call Nic and let him know?"

Selena opened her purse and pulled out a compact. Flipping it open, she powered her nose. "Nobody was happy having Richie underfoot—not even Richie. I thought it would be best if he found somewhere else to stay."

"He was *thirteen,* Selena."

"He was fourteen by then."

"Big deal. Fourteen is still too young to wander the streets."

"I admit I should have called Nic or something, but I didn't. No harm was done, anyway. Nic hired a detective and Richie was found." She snapped the compact shut and slipped it back into her slim purse.

"No wonder Nic doesn't trust you or anyone else," Jane muttered.

"What did you say?"

"Nothing."

"I suppose you think I'm horrid for not begging Richie to stay, but you didn't know him back then. He couldn't talk without using obscenities. I think he was on drugs."

"His parents had died," Jane reminded her. "He was dealing with grief and shock and being a teenager."

"You didn't live with him, Jane. You can't know what a nightmare it was."

Deciding to drop the subject, Jane tried to reconcile the rebellious youth with the soft-spoken young man she'd met at Nic's. Richie certainly wasn't the first or the last rebel who had become a responsible adult.

"You wouldn't even know him now," Jane said. "He's polite and compassionate and very bright."

"I'm glad he made something of himself," Selena said, although she didn't sound interested. She glanced out the window. "We're at the courthouse. God, how I dread this. It will take all my control not to spit in Nic's face when I see him."

The chauffeur dropped them in front of the courthouse, then went to find a parking space. Jane and Selena mounted the stone steps and went inside. Checking with an information clerk, they took the elevator to the second floor and the appointed courtroom.

Selena's attorney greeted them, then took her into a private room to go over their strategy. Jane sat on a hard bench at the far end of the hallway and listened to voices echo and footsteps ping against the marble floor. She felt Nic's presence before she looked up to see him striding confidently toward her. A smile touched his mouth. He wore an expensive, expertly tailored, dark blue suit, white shirt and red striped tie. He looked like the Nicolas Thunderheart of old, the image of the man she'd developed a crush on. His hair was brushed to a high sheen and he'd trimmed it so that it barely brushed the top of his collar.

She longed for her Tarzan Tonto.

Jane's heart stopped beating for a few moments, then thundered to life again. Inexplicably, she wanted to cry.

"Hello, Lady Jane," he said, sitting beside her on the bench. "Where's your wicked sister?"

"In with her lawyer." Jane looked around. "Where's your legal eagle?"

"Downstairs in another hearing. He's a busy boy today." Nicolas checked his watch. "Our hearing won't convene for at least a half hour. The judge is running late."

"Oh." Jane took a deep breath. "In that case, how about stepping outside with me? I'd like to talk to you without hearing my echo."

"Sounds like a plan." He slipped the fingers of one hand through hers. "One last-ditch effort to make me see reason?"

Jane shook her head. "I just want to talk, Nicolas. It might be our last chance before all hell breaks loose."

He sent her a chiding frown. "I don't intend to bloody Selena, Jane. I might live in the wild, but I'm not a wild man."

"Sometimes I wonder..."

They took the stairs and went out a side door to a sunny plaza. She and Nicolas sat on a cold, iron bench under a bare-branched elm. Squirrels chattered and pigeons cooed and pecked at the ground around them.

Jane pulled her wool coat more securely around her. Tipping back her head, she let the sunlight pour over her face and ease her tension headache. "It's been a bad couple of weeks."

"You still hate me?"

"I don't hate you," she said emotionlessly. "Sometimes, however, I wish I'd never met you."

Jane gasped when his hands locked on her upper arms and he twisted her around to face him. His eyes seemed to burn and his mouth pulled taut.

"Don't say that, Jane. Can't you understand why I can't trust Selena?"

"I'm beginning to understand... hey, ease up. You don't know your own strength."

He seemed puzzled, then his hands popped off her arms as if he'd been scorched. "I'm sorry. I didn't mean..." Running both hands over his hair, he rested them on top of his head and looked stricken, as if his emotions were suddenly overflowing and he couldn't do a damn thing to stop them.

"Aw, hell, I don't know what I mean anymore." He squeezed his eyes shut. "All I know is that I miss you every night, every day, every god-awful hour, and that I want Mandy in my life." He removed his hands from his head and a rebellious lock of his dark hair broke loose from the carefully brushed styling.

Jane's heart cried for him and she fingered the stray lock, letting it cling to her finger. His mouth looked too tense, too unhappy. She leaned forward and placed her lips lightly against his, then forced herself away from him.

"Selena and I talked about what life was like when Richie lived with you. She told me about the day he ran away."

A wariness tensed the skin around his eyes. Sliding one arm along the back of the bench, he stared moodily at a dry fountain in the near distance. "Bet she didn't tell you everything."

"She said she didn't let you know Richie had left and that she didn't try to stop him."

His eyebrows jumped up. "Well, well. She came clean. I'm surprised."

"That's when you learned not to trust her."

"Oh, I figured that out before then, but that pretty much closed the book on her."

"And you learned not to trust Prescott when he admitted in court he'd lied to you and everyone else."

"Right, although I should have seen that coming long before then."

"But I can't pinpoint when you learned not to trust me."

He pursed his lips, and she knew he was kicking himself for having stepped in her trap. He eyed her with open apprehension.

"Could you enlighten me?"

He shook his head.

"So is Richie right? You don't trust anyone?"

"Jane, it isn't about trust—"

"Yes, it is, Nicolas. I asked you to let me handle this. I promised I would do everything possible to find a peaceful solution to this problem. I implored you to give me a little time to make Selena see how you'd changed and that you'd be a good guardian and parent to Mandy. I pleaded with you not to jump the gun because it was important to me that Mandy not be bounced around in the court system."

He sighed heavily and his eyelids drooped. "I did what I thought was best. Mandy's not going to be bounced around. She's not here today, is she?"

"No."

"Then she won't even know the details of this, unless Selena or you tell her." He smiled faintly. "Has she mentioned me, asked about me?"

"Yes, of course. She has a father, so she's curious and excited. She's told all her friends about you." Jane laughed. "You should have heard her telling Mom, as if you and Mom had never met."

"In a way, we haven't."

Jane nodded, following his train of thought. "Yes, I bet Mom would be the first to admit you've changed. When I told her you were more interested in birds than in the stock market, she said it sure didn't sound like the career-minded son-in-law she once had."

"Actually, I'm still interested in the stock market, but it's not my obsession." He laughed softly. "I've spent a lot of time lately planning activities for me and Mandy. I even went to the elementary school open house. I've been to it before, of course, but this time I looked at it with the eyes of a parent."

"Did it stack up?"

"Yes." He chuckled. "It's good enough for my daughter." Tilting his head to one side, he grinned. "My daughter. God, that sounds wonderful. And she's such a great kid." His face reflected his pride. "She's so smart and cute. Do you think she looks like me? Not that I'm cute, but I think she has a few of my features."

"A few? Yes, I'd say so. And you *are* cute. Especially right this minute."

He swung his gaze to hers. Within a blink of time, desire flamed in his eyes. "I don't suppose you'd let me kiss you right this minute, would you?"

She thought to refuse, but what slipped from her lips was "Yes."

The touch of his mouth, so familiar, so thrilling, triggered a deep yearning within her and she realized she'd been afraid she'd never be kissed by him again. The possibility that this might be the last kiss they shared spurred her on, encouraging her to open herself to him and run her hands over his mussed hair. She flattened her breasts against the muscled wall of his chest and scooted closer to him on the bench, uncaring that others might be watching.

He was the one to end the kiss, tearing his mouth from hers, his breathing ragged and hoarse.

He scanned her face with hungry eyes and probed the corners of her stinging mouth with fingers that trembled slightly. "One touch, one kiss, and we're panting for each other. Never in my life has a woman affected me as you do, Jane Litton. I want you, I need you..." His lips stamped hers again.

"Ah, but do you trust me?"

He grimaced. "Jane, no, not that again."

She clamped her hands over his on either side of her head and made him look her in the eyes. "Nicolas, if only you'd try. If you can't trust me, then what hope do we have of any real love between us?"

"Don't say that."

"It's true."

"I can fight for only one relationship at a time, Jane. I'm fighting for Mandy today."

"There doesn't have to be a fight, Nicolas."

He smiled sadly. "You're naive."

"You're jaded." She stood. "We should go back inside. We've been out here about half an hour."

He rose from the bench, tall and lean. A familiar stranger.

"Better wipe my lipstick off your mouth," she advised.

He used his white handkerchief to remove the smear of passion pink.

Inside the courthouse again, they walked side by side without speaking. As they approached the courtroom, someone called out to them. Jane looked down the hall to a grouping of three men and Selena. Her sister scowled at her, displeased to see that Jane was conspiring with the enemy.

"What's up?" Nicolas asked as they neared the group.

"Where have you been?" Selena demanded of Jane.

"Outside." Jane recognized one of the men as Selena's lawyer.

"Mr. Thunderheart?" one of the others held out his hand. "I'm Davis Johnson, one of Judge Reincomb's assistants. She has asked that you, Mrs. D'Mato and your attorneys meet in this ante chamber and try to come up with a settlement without the court's intervention." The man waited a moment to let this sink in. "Would you be agreeable to this?"

Nicolas glanced at his attorney, then shrugged. "I guess. What do you think, Selena? Would it be like spitting in the wind?"

Selena tipped up her chin. "I've already agreed. *I* was here on time, waiting for you. I thought Jane had been kidnapped."

"Fine," Davis Johnson said, already taking Selena by the elbow. "The ante chamber is right here. You can go on inside. I'll be right across the hall in that office. When you've reached an agreement, or if you find you must have the court's intervention, then just let me know." He opened the door to a small room where a table and six chairs took up most of the space. "There is a pitcher of water and glasses on the table. Help yourself. No smoking, please."

Jane held back, realizing she had no place here. Selena strode inside, followed by her lawyer. Nic's attorney went next. Nic paused, glancing at Jane.

"Aren't you coming in?"

"No." Jane sighed. "I'd only make things worse in there probably."

One corner of his mouth quirked in a hesitant grin. "Probably. Wish me luck?"

He started to go inside, but she grabbed his lapels and pulled him toward her, then backed him against the wall. Startled by her manhandling, he laughed softly, his eyes going wide.

"What's this?"

"Nic, listen to me," Jane whispered, her urgency slicing through to him and killing his amusement. "Please, listen."

He nodded, his hands moving up to cover hers. "Go on, Lady Jane. I'm listening."

She breathed easier. "Tell Selena you're dropping the petition, but you hope she will grant you joint custody because you trust her judgment."

"Jane..."

"No, be quiet. Just listen for a change." She sucked in a breath and stood on tiptoe to be nearly eye level with him. "I know her better than you do, Nicolas. All she wants is to feel as if she had a say-so in this—that this was her decision to make as a mother for her child. Don't strip her of this, or you'll be fighting a battle no one will win." She unfisted her hands and smoothed his lapels. His fingers caressed hers. She decided to speak a language he would understand.

"Nic, please invest your trust in me. I promise it will pay big dividends. I want Mandy to be nurtured by both her mother and father, to be wanted and loved by both. Not to be a bone of contention between them."

"Mr. Thunderheart?" Nic's attorney stepped out and looked curiously at them.

"In a minute," Nic growled, flashing the man a look that sent him back into the ante chamber.

Jane patted his shoulder. "Trust me." She backed away, giving him space, and offered a loving smile. "I have every confidence in you."

He narrowed his eyes, gazing at her intently, then shook his head. She hoped for a clear indication of his thinking, but she received none. He simply turned and went inside, closing the door behind him.

Jane sat heavily on the nearest bench, drained, her knees shaking. She glanced at her watch. It was two. How long would they be in there, and did anything she'd said to Nicolas get through his suit of armor?

MINUTES SHY of three o'clock the door opened and Nic's lawyer emerged, looking officious. He strode across the hall and summoned Davis Johnson. Jane strained, but couldn't make out their mumbled words. Johnson and the attorney went back inside to the ante chamber.

"Mr. Thunderheart?" she heard Johnson say. "If you'll come with me, please? This won't take long, but we have to make it all official and legal, you understand."

Nic came out, glanced at Jane, gave a wincing smile, then strode with the two other men down the hall and around a corner. She jumped to her feet. *What had happened?*

Poking her head around the door frame, she got a view of Selena's attorney arranging papers in a briefcase. "Where's my sister?"

Selena slinked around the door. "Here I am. I was freshening my makeup in this wall mirror. We're done here. Ready to go?"

"Then you don't have to see the judge?"

"No." She smiled. "We settled out of court, so to speak."

Jane held her breath a second. "Is that good?"

Selena laughed. "Yes, it's *very* good. Anytime you don't have to stand in front of a judge and spill your guts for public record, it's very good, indeed."

"Amen," her attorney tacked on as he brushed past Selena. "I'll send you the necessary paperwork for your signature as soon as I get it. Until then, you'll be hearing from me."

"Yes, as in, the bill's in the mail," Selena drawled with a slow wink. "Thanks again, Norman, darling."

"This time I didn't have to do anything. My kind of court action." The attorney nodded a farewell to Jane, then hurried from the room.

"So tell me what happened," Jane enthused.

"It was totally unexpected. Nic's attorney started to drone on and on about a father's rights and how Nic's been denied his fatherhood for lo, these many years..." She rolled her eyes expressively. "Poor, little Nic, and all that garbage."

"Except that it's *not* garbage," Jane said, unable to stop herself from defending him.

Selena placed one hand on her jutting hip. "Am I telling this or are you?"

"Go ahead."

"Very well. There's always a critic around," she fussed. "Anyway, as I was saying, Nic's attorney was boring everyone to distraction when Nic suddenly cut him off and said that he was withdrawing the petition. Well! His attorney looked at him as if he'd gone loony, but Nic was dead serious. Can you beat that?"

"Remarkable." It was all Jane could do not to perform a happy dance, which would give Selena cause to wonder if going loony was contagious.

"His attorney started sputtering, but Nic was adamant. He said he was withdrawing the petition, but he hoped I would grant him joint custody of our daughter. He left it up to me, can you believe that?" Selena shook her head. "Why didn't he do that in the first place? Why drag us to the courthouse and through all this high drama? God, the past few weeks have been unbearable. The big fathead."

"Maybe he wanted to see you, Selena. It's been a long time, you know. He probably saw for himself how you'd changed and he figured he could trust you to do what's best for Mandy—for all of you."

Selena nodded and glanced around at the small room. "Maybe you're right. Let's get out of here." Moving out to the wide hallway, she shook herself, as if getting rid of bad vibes. "It's over. I'm so glad it's over."

"What did you decide?" Jane asked.

"I asked him to give me time to think about it. I wanted to talk to you and Mother and Jerome first before I gave my approval." She smiled cunningly. "That bowled him over. I could tell he thought I'd hem and haw, but I informed him I'd let him know within a month. That seemed to suit him." She looked down at her stylish, black leather heels. "We talked about...lots of things. Water under-the-bridge things. You're right. He's changed. He's more sensitive, more caring. I could tell he truly adores Amanda. And, naturally, he's all she talks about lately."

"Little girls should always be in love with their daddies."

Selena regarded Jane and she placed an arm around her shoulders. "You deserved a good daddy, little sis. Is that why you've been so *intrusive* of late?"

Jane laughed along with Selena. "Yes, I suppose it all boils down to that—and the fact I also adore Mandy."

"Excuse me?"

Jane and Selena turned to face the woman who'd interrupted them. She was in her forties, plump and smiling shyly.

"Are you...that is, you're Selena Carr, the opera singer, aren't you?"

Selena preened. "Why, yes, I am."

"Oh, how exciting. I love you!" the woman gushed, presenting a pen and a bank deposit slip. "I don't have anything but this to write on, but would you? Please sign it so that I can prove to my husband I met you. He'll be so jealous! We're both huge fans of yours."

"Isn't that nice." Selena took the paper and pen from her and signed her name with a dramatic flourish. "There you are, dear."

"We saw you last week on the education channel. Live at Lincoln Center. You did that piece from Verdi."

"That's right."

"And it was magnificent! Are you performing in Dallas now?"

"No, I live here part of the time."

"Yes, I've read that in the newspaper."

"Thank you for your kind words," Selena said, already sidling away. "Please excuse us. We must be going."

"Oh, sure. Thanks for the autograph. You're beautiful, too! A face like a goddess!"

"You're too kind," Selena called over her shoulder, ushering Jane along with her as they headed for the stairwell.

"Wow." Jane whistled low. "You're famous."

"Well, of course, I am. I'm Selena Carr, you dunce."

Laughing, they found themselves on the main floor. Selena headed for the door, but Jane held her back.

"Where did Nic go?"

"He had to sign some papers of some sort, dropping the petition, I think."

"Oh." Jane wanted to wait for him, but she didn't know where he'd gone in the maze of corridors and offices.

"My feet are killing me. These heels aren't broken in yet. Jane, be a dear and track down the limo driver for me. He should be parked nearby...somewhere."

"My, my, aren't we the haughty opera star," Jane observed, then grinned. "Okay. Save your dogs. I wore my cheap fake-leather pumps, so I'm in no pain." She paused and gripped Selena's arm. "You *will* agree to the joint custody, right? You won't play with Nic's feelings."

"Of course, but I want to tell Jerome first."

"You mean, you want to tell him that boarding school is no longer an option."

"Yes. He'll be fine with it."

"Right. He just doesn't want Mandy traveling with you two."

"It isn't a good life for a child," Selena snapped.

"You're right. Jerome's right," Jane placated. She scanned the area, hoping to catch sight of a tall, dark and handsome man in a three-piece suit. "Don't leave Nic hanging very long. He's been agonizing over this, same as you."

"I'll tell him soon enough." Selena sighed. "What are you looking for? Or, rather, *who* are you looking for?"

"I... well, I thought I'd say goodbye."

"That's a word I don't think you want to say to him, little sis."

Startled, Jane could only stare at Selena. She felt her cheeks warm with embarrassment.

"I think he's in love with you, Jane," Selena said, her voice soft, her smile comforting. "If you want to pursue this, you have my blessing."

Shock consumed her. A few moments passed before she could find her voice. "Selena, I don't know what to say."

"You don't have to say anything." Selena bussed her hot cheek. "Tarzan and Jane. Together again." Giving her a little push, she laughed. "Go find the chauffeur before someone else recognizes me and makes me sign a grocery list.''

Jane hugged Selena fiercely, stunned by her sister's generosity and sense of fair play. ''You're a marvel, you know that? Okay, okay, I'm going.'' Jane dashed out onto the busy street, into the gentle, winter sunlight. Suddenly, it was a beautiful day and everyone around her seemed to be laughing. Everyone around her seemed to be in love. Just like her.

Chapter Fifteen

A light snow fell through the bare-branched trees and settled on the evergreens' outstretched arms. Jane's feet landed softly on the frozen ground, while all around her the wind sighed, eddying and swirling the delicate white flakes. Pausing on the trail, obliterated by the snow covering but clearly etched in her mind, Jane looked up at the swaying tops of the firs and Scotch pine. Flakes touched her lashes, became trapped and melted. She breathed deeply, filling her lungs with the sharp, cold air.

She loved it here in these Smokies.

Too soon a chill reached her bones and she shifted her backpack to a more comfortable position against her spine, preparing to move on. Something brown and big teased her periphery vision and she glanced sideways. Her breath whistled down her throat and the chill within her grew more intense. Her teeth chattered and she bit her tongue, which brought tears to her eyes. Her instincts told her to retreat, but before her feet could answer the request, she recognized the man dressed all in buckskin standing motionless a few feet from her.

"Nicolas!" Her heart resumed its normal beat. "You scared me. I thought...I thought..." Words scattered to the four winds as her eyes feasted on Nicolas Thunderheart, his big, rangy body clad in buttery, fringed buckskin. He grasped a long rifle in one hand. Bits of leaves and grass dotted his dark hair. Stubble shadowed his chin and jaws.

The return of Tarzan Tonto, she thought. Longing pumped through her, firing her blood and making her heart race.

"You thought what?" he asked, his voice a deep purr that made her knees tremble.

"Oh, forget what I thought."

Two long strides erased the distance between them and she was in his arms; the rifle fell to the ground, forgotten. Nic's hands roamed her waist and hips. He stroked her lips with his tongue and then surged inside, deepening the kiss, staking his claim.

Lifting his mouth from hers, he framed her face in his hands and tipped it up to his. "You're trespassing again, lady."

"Shoot me." She kissed his scratchy chin and ran her thumbs across his high cheekbones. "Merry Christmas."

"Do you bring glad tidings?"

She knew he was teasing, but the implication doused some of her holiday spirit. He must have sensed her dampened mood because his hands tightened slightly and his gaze sharpened on her.

"You *have* brought news of Selena's decision, haven't you?"

Jane plucked dried grass and a leaf from his hair, then escaped his embrace. She knew she shouldn't be so sensitive to his every nuance, but she couldn't help it. She wanted him to want her with no strings attached.

"What if I haven't brought news? Would I still be welcome?" She glanced at the rifle lying on the snowy ground. "Will you shoot the messenger if I displease you?"

"Don't be ridiculous." He retrieved the rifle and rubbed the snow off it.

Jane regarded him, a smile playing at the corners of her mouth. "What are you doing in that outfit? Another historical rendezvous?"

"No, I was hunting."

"For what?"

"Pheasant, quail, wild turkey." He held his arms out from his sides. "You like?"

"Me like, Tonto." She stepped closer and ran the flat of her hands across the soft buckskin covering his wide chest. Laces crisscrossed in a deep V neck, the ends hanging loose and untied. She gave them a tug. "Makes me remember the first time I saw you out here. I thought I was going to be your prey that day."

"You were, and you were hard to bring down."

"Do you think the chase is over?" She laughed reproachfully. "I'm still free as a bird."

He lifted one dark brow. "Are you going to keep me in suspense? I'd like to know if Selena sent you."

Jane turned away from him, wishing he was interested in her feelings and not so wrapped up in Selena's decision. Of course, that was selfish of her. Mandy was on his mind and that was only natural.

"I came on my own. Selena will be here tomorrow afternoon."

He frowned. "Why is she coming here?"

"She would have asked for permission to visit, but it's not like she could pick up a phone and give you a ring." Giving in to a twinge of sympathy, she reached for one of his hands and squeezed his fingers. "Selena's bringing Jerome and Amanda with her. She and Jerome will leave the day after Christmas, but Amanda stays here, at least until sometime in January."

He stared at her, his eyes widening, then he rocked his head back in a burst of joy, his face lighting up with a beaming smile. "Thank God," he whispered. Righting his head, he bestowed a soft kiss on Jane's lips. "She agreed? She's giving me joint custody?"

"I told you she would, didn't I?"

"Thank you, Jane. From the bottom of my heart, I thank you." He stroked a hand over her wool knit cap and kissed her forehead. "You're shivering."

"Yes, I'm chilled, and my tongue hurts."

"Pardon me?" He gave her a bemused smile.

"I must have bit it accidently when I saw you." She touched the tender place. "You don't have any plans for Christmas, do you? I'm not interrupting you?"

"It's been hard to get into the spirit. I'm glad you're here. Come on. I was going to decorate the tree after I bagged some fowl, but the hunt can wait. I need to get you into my warm house so that your teeth will stop chattering." He slipped his arm around her waist and guided her through the forest. "How about a cup of cocoa?"

"Sounds heavenly." She smiled at him, happy to be in his company again. "What Christmas plans have you made?"

"I'm decking the halls and wrapping presents for my loved ones. I was hoping Mandy would visit sometime during the holidays and I wanted to be ready, just in case. I placed my faith in you, and I assumed you'd come through as you promised."

"You trusted me."

"Was there ever a doubt?"

She gave him a playful punch in the side. "Very funny. I think doubt is your middle name." A thought struck her. "Hey, what *is* your middle name?"

"Tonto," he jested.

Laughing, she moved with him through the softly falling, footsteps muffled. His arm around her waist gave her a sense of security. He smelled of leather and earth, of forest and winter. Jane slipped her arms around his middle and leaned her cheek against him. The leather was as soft as chamois, the man it clothed as tough as jerky.

"I'm taking a vacation from my work until after the holidays."

"Great." He hugged her closer. "We'll have a great time. You and me and Mandy."

Jane moved ahead of him into the clearing. Seeing the house through a curtain of snow made it even more beautiful to her eyes. The stream gurgled beneath it, a cold gray color with whitecaps. Lacy snow drifted across the house's roof. Columns of smoke poured from the chimneys. She caught Nic looking at her, a puzzled expression on his face.

"Every time I see this place, I get a little thrill," she confessed. "Every season makes it look different."

He took her by the hand. "This is going to be a special Christmas, thanks to you."

The house was redolent with the scents of cinnamon and pine. Just as he had during her first visit, Nic helped her remove her backpack and left it on the table in the mudroom. Upstairs on the main floor she surveyed the bright trappings of Christmas strewn hither and yon.

The floor was littered with tinsel, huge red bows and sprigs of mistletoe. A freshly cut Douglas fir, wearing a dozen strings of lights, dominated the center of the living room. Flames danced and crackled in the fireplace and Jane gingerly crossed the room to stand in front of it. She held out her hands to the warmth and sighed.

"Ah, that feels lovely. Where's that hot cocoa?"

"Coming right up, ma'am." He ducked into the kitchen.

"I suppose your brother is visiting his soon-to-be in-laws," she called to him.

"That's right. I'll send him a telegram after the holidays and tell him about Mandy. He's anxious to meet her."

She heard his deep chuckle. "What's so funny?"

"Oh, I've been having a good time teasing him," he called to her. "I told him that you refer to him as 'Peewee' now that you've seen his endowments."

Jane sucked in a breath and went into the kitchen. Nic stirred cocoa in a pot, an evil grin on his face. "You didn't! Nicolas, thanks to you, Richie and I will turn beet red next time we see each other."

"I'll tell him I've been joshing him before then." He turned off the stove burner under the pot and poured the contents into two mugs.

Jane took one of them. "You're incorrigible."

"I know." He smiled proudly and escorted her back into the warm living room.

He sat on the couch, but Jane strolled around the room and peeked into the boxes of decorations. Kneeling at one of them, she examined a cut-crystal star for the top of the tree and sniffed at vanilla and cherry scented candles. Boughs of holly graced the fireplace mantel. Sparkling lights framed the big windows. A plate of gingerbread sat on the coffee table. She helped herself to a square of it and took a big bite as she joined Nic on the couch.

"Delicious," she said, her mouth full of the cake.

"Thanks. I baked it this morning."

She sipped the cocoa and sighed with pleasure. "I'm warm and my tongue isn't hurting anymore. I'm a happy camper." Her gaze rested on the emerald-colored fir. "I love your tree. It's going to be beautiful."

He took the mug and cake from her and set them both on the table. Jane had only a moment to ponder his intent before he gathered her against him, his arms enfolding her. His kiss stole her breath and her equilibrium.

"Nic, wait a minute." She was proud of herself for finding a modicum of self-will and squirming out of his embrace. "I'm glad you missed me, but give me a minute to get my bearings."

He crossed his arms against his chest and sat back on the couch, looking for all the world like a little boy who'd had his hand slapped. "You obviously haven't been as miserable as I've been without you."

"Nicolas, will you listen to yourself? I've only been here fifteen minutes." She peeked at him from beneath her lashes. "Did you really miss me?"

"Oh, hell, no," he groused, then pushed up from the couch. Stalking to the windows, he stared out at the golden bars of sunlight falling through the branches. "When the wind whistles around the house, I hear your voice. When the breeze touches my skin, I remember your hands on me. When I look at this land now, I see only loneliness without you." His green eyes found her, pinned her. "I ache for you, Jane."

She drew in a trembling breath. "And I for you." She held up a detaining hand when he started toward her. "But we have more obstacles than most people."

"Are you worried about how Selena will react to us being together?"

"She already knows and she's given me her blessing." She picked up her mug and blew at the steam rising from the cocoa.

"She knows?" He blinked in surprise. "She didn't give you grief over it?"

"Yes, a little, but now she's okay with it."

"Amazing."

"Selena is full of surprises." Catching his gaze, she smiled. "But then, so are you. I was so glad when you took my advice at the courthouse. I sent you a fax saying just that . . . did you ever get it?"

"Yes. And I got the two you sent after that. Did you get mine?"

She nodded, feeling color paint her cheeks. His had been more intimate, asking her to come to him, no matter what, telling her how he needed to know they could patch up their differences. Hers had merely stated her relief at his decision and asked him to hold tight. Selena and Jerome were discussing their schedules and would be contacting him soon.

"I know a good thing when I see it." He moved away from the windows and sat on the edge of the coffee table. "You've restored my trust in others. That's a precious Christmas gift. Come to think of it, you're responsible for me getting to know Mandy, too, which is another tremendous gift. How can I ever thank you enough, Jane? It's impossible."

"Just be a good father to Mandy. Be the father to her I never had."

He reached out to stroke his fingertips down her cheek. "I'll do my best."

Blinking back sentimental tears, Jane switched her attention to the fir. "Like I said before, nice tree."

He nodded. "I've had my eye on it since June."

"Did you use a saw or just push it over with your brute strength?"

He laughed. "Will you help me decorate it?"

"Of course. Mandy likes strings of popcorn and lots of tinsel."

''What do *you* like?''

She brought her gaze back to his. ''You, in leather.'' Before he could make a move, Jane sprang up and paced to the fireplace. ''Mandy's excited about coming here. She's telling all her friends what a cool dad she has. I think Jerome's even a little jealous.''

He grinned. ''So I'm a cool dad, huh? I like that.''

''You and Mandy are going to be great together, Nicolas.'' Jane drew in a breath, trying to ease the tension knotting in her chest. She hated the indecision and doubt deviling her. Did he want her for the same reasons she wanted him? Mandy fitted into his life, but where would she fit? Did she come with the family package or did Nicolas Thunderheart truly love her and need her beyond helping Mandy bond to him?

''So you're on vacation.'' He stretched to his feet, standing almost as tall as the fir tree. ''In your line of work, can you design your creations just about anywhere?''

''Yes.'' A quivering found her heart. ''Well, anywhere with a drafting table, good light, some jewelry tools and few distractions.''

''Then you could work here, right?''

''Yes, but I don't want to work. I'm on vacation.''

He nodded brusquely. ''After your vacation.''

She gave a quick shrug, her nerves aflutter. What was he asking? Forever or a day? He walked toward her, stopping a scant inch in front of her. Caressing her arms from shoulder to wrist, he took her hands within his. Jane released a long, simmering sigh. Oh, how easily he could manipulate her. It was truly disarming.

''Would you like to stay past the New Year?''

"For Mandy?" It was out before she could stop it.

"Is that what you think, Jane? You believe I only want you here to baby-sit Mandy?"

"You said my being here would make the transition easier."

"Sure, but that's not the only reason I want you here."

She stood perfectly still, waiting, hoping, refusing to lead him into a conversation if he didn't want to go.

"Now that we have this custody thing behind us, I thought we could move forward." His thumbs smoothed across the tops of her hands. "Isn't that what you want?"

She swallowed the lump in her throat. "What do you want, Nicolas?"

"You."

"Me, you've had."

A smile tugged at his lips. "True. I want you all the time. Here. Beside me." He looked at her more intently. "Has something happened? Is there someone else?"

"No." She slumped and rested her forehead on his chin. "There's only you."

"Good." His arms came around her. "Because I need you and I won't share. Life without you has become unbearable. I wanted to ask you to marry me, but I was afraid you'd give me a lecture about taking marriage seriously and how it's not something one jumps into and that I should have learned that when I married Selena—"

"Yes," she said, lifting her head to look at him, her heart soaring into her throat. "Yes, I will."

He blinked. "You will..." His eyes widened. "Marry me, you mean?"

"Yes." She smiled. "I hope you were serious."

"Sure, I am, but...are *you* serious?"

Laughing, she looped her arms around his neck. "Yes, yes, yes. If you're sure, that is. I don't want to rush you into anything and I don't want you to marry me for convenience or anything like that."

"How about if I marry you because I would like to make love to you twenty-four hours a day if humanly possible?"

"That's a good enough reason. I feel the same way."

"I love you. You know that, right?"

"I wasn't convinced until now. I see the evidence in your eyes. You do love me." She sighed as if world-weary. "You're a hard man to pin down, Nicolas."

He spun her around before setting her on her feet again. Happiness bubbled in his voice. "This has to be fate, our falling in love, because it's too screwy to be anything else."

Jane doubled over laughing, her eyes tearing. When she got control of her giggles, she stared at something shiny, something beautiful, something every woman dreams of.

"An engagement ring," she whispered, stunned.

Nic lifted her left hand and slipped the ring on her finger. "I took a chance. If you want to design your own, I'll understand."

"No, oh, no." She stared at the pear-shaped diamond in a simple gold setting. "I would rather that you pick it out. Oh, Nicolas, it's the most fabulous ring in the world."

He grinned. "I'm glad you approve. I didn't know if your taste ran to simple or ornate."

"I love this." She kissed him tenderly. "I'll design yours, okay?"

"Okay. You'll have plenty of time. I want a long engagement. I want to plan this wedding. I want to make up a guest list and send out invitations. I want to get married here, on my... our land, if that's all right with you."

She laughed at his enthusiasm. "You're determined to get it right this time, huh?"

"You bet. This time I've got the right woman." A teasing light entered his eyes. "Or, rather, the right sister."

"By long... just what do you mean? Months? Years?"

"Years, no. I was thinking about a June wedding."

"How traditional." She stared at the ring, moving her finger so the cuts caught the light. "I believe I can hold out that long before I get the band that matches this."

He dipped his head and kissed her slowly, leisurely. As the kisses deepened, Jane made a move toward the couch, but her foot got tangled in a pile of garlands and she lost her balance. Nic tried to catch her, but he stepped back into a box of tinsel and fell, his rump hitting the floor before she landed on top of him.

Laughing, they rolled in each other's arms across holly boughs and mistletoe, garland and twinkle lights. Jane's laughter dwindled to a contented sigh as she stared down into Nic's face, her body resting atop his.

"Merry Christmas, Lady Jane."

She kissed his eyelids, his cheekbones, his mouth. "You can unwrap me now."

"You don't think we should wait until tomorrow to unwrap our gifts?"

She shook her head vigorously.

"You sure?" he teased.

Jane kissed him hard and rocked her hips against him. His hands covered her backside and she felt his purely masculine response. Tearing her mouth from his, she gazed into the green fire of his eyes.

"Trust me," she whispered, and he proved once again that he did.

AMERICAN ❖ ROMANCE®

"Whether you want him for business...or pleasure, for one month or for one night, we have the husband you've been looking for. When circumstances dictate the need for the appearance of a man in your life, call 1-800-HUSBAND for an uncomplicated, uncompromising solution. Call now.
Operators are standing by...."

I ♥ 800 HUSBAND

Pick up the phone—along with five desperate singles—and enter the Harrington Agency, where no one lacks a perfect mate. Only thing is, there's no guarantee this will stay a business arrangement....

For five fun-filled frolics with the mate of your dreams, catch all the 1-800-HUSBAND books:

> #596 COUNTERFEIT HUSBAND
> by Linda Randall Wisdom in August
> #597 HER TWO HUSBANDS
> by Mollie Molay in September
> #601 THE LAST BRIDESMAID
> by Leandra Logan in October
> #605 THE COWBOY HIRES A WIFE
> by Jenna McKnight in November
> #609 THE CHRISTMAS HUSBAND
> by Mary Anne Wilson in December

Coming to you only from American Romance!

HFH-1

OFFICIAL RULES

FLYAWAY VACATION SWEEPSTAKES 3449

NO PURCHASE OR OBLIGATION NECESSARY

Three Harlequin Reader Service 1995 shipments will contain respectively, coupons for entry into three different prize drawings, one for a trip for two to San Francisco, another for a trip for two to Las Vegas and the third for a trip for two to Orlando, Florida. To enter any drawing using an Entry Coupon, simply complete and mail according to directions.

There is no obligation to continue using the Reader Service to enter and be eligible for any prize drawing. You may also enter any drawing by hand printing the words "Flyaway Vacation," your name and address on a 3"x5" card and the destination of the prize you wish that entry to be considered for (i.e., San Francisco trip, Las Vegas trip or Orlando trip). Send your 3"x5" entries via first-class mail (limit: one entry per envelope) to: Flyaway Vacation Sweepstakes 3449, c/o Prize Destination you wish that entry to be considered for, P.O. Box 1315, Buffalo, NY 14269-1315, USA or P.O. Box 610, Fort Erie, Ontario L2A 5X3, Canada.

To be eligible for the San Francisco trip, entries must be received by 5/30/95; for the Las Vegas trip, 7/30/95; and for the Orlando trip, 9/30/95.

Winners will be determined in random drawings conducted under the supervision of D.L. Blair, Inc., an independent judging organization whose decisions are final, from among all eligible entries received for that drawing. San Francisco trip prize includes round-trip airfare for two, 4-day/3-night weekend accommodations at a first-class hotel, and $500 in cash (trip must be taken between 7/30/95—7/30/96, approximate prize value—$3,500); Las Vegas trip includes round-trip airfare for two, 4-day/3-night weekend accommodations at a first-class hotel, and $500 in cash (trip must be taken between 9/30/95—9/30/96, approximate prize value—$3,500); Orlando trip includes round-trip airfare for two, 4-day/3-night weekend accommodations at a first-class hotel, and $500 in cash (trip must be taken between 11/30/95—11/30/96, approximate prize value—$3,500). All travelers must sign and return a Release of Liability prior to travel. Hotel accommodations and flights are subject to accommodation and schedule availability. Sweepstakes open to residents of the U.S. (except Puerto Rico) and Canada, 18 years of age or older. Employees and immediate family members of Harlequin Enterprises, Ltd., D.L. Blair, Inc., their affiliates, subsidiaries and all other agencies, entities and persons connected with the use, marketing or conduct of this sweepstakes are not eligible. Odds of winning a prize are dependent upon the number of eligible entries received for that drawing. Prize drawing and winner notification for each drawing will occur no later than 15 days after deadline for entry eligibility for that drawing. Limit: one prize to an individual, family or organization. All applicable laws and regulations apply. Sweepstakes offer void wherever prohibited by law. Any litigation within the province of Quebec respecting the conduct and awarding of the prizes in this sweepstakes must be submitted to the Regies des loteries et Courses du Quebec. In order to win a prize, residents of Canada will be required to correctly answer a time-limited arithmetical skill-testing question. Value of prizes are in U.S. currency.

Winners will be obligated to sign and return an Affidavit of Eligibility within 30 days of notification. In the event of noncompliance within this time period, prize may not be awarded. If any prize or prize notification is returned as undeliverable, that prize will not be awarded. By acceptance of a prize, winner consents to use of his/her name, photograph or other likeness for purposes of advertising, trade and promotion on behalf of Harlequin Enterprises, Ltd., without further compensation, unless prohibited by law.

For the names of prizewinners (available after 12/31/95), send a self-addressed, stamped envelope to: Flyaway Vacation Sweepstakes 3449 Winners, P.O. Box 4200, Blair, NE 68009.

RVC KAL